Christm...

Gifts are ...
hold in your ... ...ate
at Christmas ... born in a
stable, though the ... ...ds and the wise men
did manage to bring presents as well.

These books also celebrate Christmas,
and each deals with a different gift,
the kind that can bring immeasurable love
and contentment down the years—
which we wish for all of you.

Enjoy!

Margaret O'Neill started scribbling at four and began nursing at twenty. She contracted TB and, when recovered, did her British Tuberculosis Association nursing training before general training at the Royal Portsmouth Hospital. She married, had two children, and with her late husband she owned and managed several nursing homes. Now retired and living in Sussex, she still has many nursing contacts. Her husband would have been delighted to see her books in print.

Recent titles by the same author:

NURSE FRIDAY
A FAMILY CONCERN

WRAPPED IN TINSEL

BY
MARGARET O'NEILL

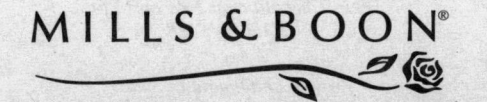

MILLS & BOON

DID YOU PURCHASE THIS BOOK WITHOUT A COVER?

If you did, you should be aware it is **stolen property** as it was reported *unsold and destroyed* by a retailer. Neither the author nor the publisher has received any payment for this book.

All the characters in this book have no existence outside the imagination of the author, and have no relation whatsoever to anyone bearing the same name or names. They are not even distantly inspired by any individual known or unknown to the author, and all the incidents are pure invention.

All Rights Reserved including the right of reproduction in whole or in part in any form. This edition is published by arrangement with Harlequin Enterprises II B.V. The text of this publication or any part thereof may not be reproduced or transmitted in any form or by any means, electronic or mechanical, including photocopying, recording, storage in an information retrieval system, or otherwise, without the written permission of the publisher.

This book is sold subject to the condition that it shall not, by way of trade or otherwise, be lent, resold, hired out or otherwise circulated without the prior consent of the publisher in any form of binding or cover other than that in which it is published and without a similar condition including this condition being imposed on the subsequent purchaser.

MILLS & BOON and MILLS & BOON with the Rose Device are registered trademarks of the publisher.

*First published in Great Britain 2000
Harlequin Mills & Boon Limited,
Eton House, 18-24 Paradise Road, Richmond, Surrey TW9 1SR*

© Margaret O'Neill 2000

ISBN 0 263 82280 X

*Set in Times Roman 10½ on 12 pt.
03-1200-43488*

*Printed and bound in Spain
by Litografía Rosés, S.A., Barcelona*

CHAPTER ONE

'WELL, you've got your wish—all that dreaming of a white Christmas has paid off,' said Marjory drily. 'There's tons of the stuff out there and, according to the local radio, The Lane is already deep in drifts. Impassable probably,' she added with a sort of gloomy relish. 'Dare say we're already cut off.'

She could be right as The Lane was the only route into Tintore, thought Nan. She looked affectionately at her secretary-cum-receptionist and laughed. 'Oh, Marge, a bit of snow makes Christmas, adds to the magic. We're all stocked up, the village store and the pharmacy are both bursting at the seams, and the kids will love it, sledging and having snowball fights. And it'll be lovely on Christmas Eve when we have the carols. Candles and lanterns and snow seem to go together—Christmas-card stuff.' Her eyes sparkled.

Like emeralds, thought Marge, astonishing herself by having such an imaginative thought. Imagination wasn't her strong suit. 'You're like a great big kid. You'd like to be out there with them, wouldn't you?' she accused, sounding severe, but a small smile touched her lips.

Nan's bubbly pleasure was infectious. And it was true about the carol service. It would be quite something, the choirboys and -girls wending their way up from the church carrying lanterns and singing, 'It came upon the midnight clear...' That was what they opened with every year. She had another extraordinarily creative thought—like medieval pilgrims in their surplices and white ruffled collars.

The phone rang. Marge was relieved—she couldn't handle any more fanciful ideas for the moment. 'Post is in your office, Matron,' she told Nan primly as she picked up the receiver. 'Good morning, Tintore Cottage Hospital,' Nan heard Marge say as she crossed the thick forest-green carpet of the entrance hall.

Dear old Marge—stiff, prim, formal or informal, she was a great friend. The rapport between them, built up over ten years, was rock solid. She was utterly dependable and totally discreet—a perfect personal secretary, though she doubled as senior receptionist much of the time when the junior receptionist was off duty.

She was relieved occasionally by Tom Barnard, porter, gardener, handyman *and* sometime receptionist. In fact, there was quite a lot of doubling up amongst the staff—it was what made the hospital tick.

Nan paused at the door of her office, a wave of pride washing over her as she surveyed the reception hall. It always looked gracious, with its elegant proportions, high ceilings, limed oak panelled walls and the wide, sweeping staircase curving up to the first floor. Now it looked festive, with a majestic Norwegian fir standing in the well of the staircase; all silver and gold, with delicate glass balls—not a plastic ornament in sight. Holly and ivy looped round the walls. It smelt festive, too, of pine and fresh greenery.

It must be the season, with all that goodwill sloshing around, she thought as tears stung the back of her eyes. How soppy can you get? Cut it out, Winters, she told herself. It was the same every year. Christmas got to her, turned her marshmallow soft.

The way everyone worked flat out to make Christmas special for the patients not well enough to go home for the holiday always amazed her, though she should have been used to it by now. She started the Christmas rota in October, and it was always filled up by the end of November. So many people seemed willing to put their own celebrations on hold so that they could help out. What other hospital could boast such a loyal and happy staff?

Most of them had worked here for years, often several members of the same family—it was almost a family concern. It was a true cottage hospital, an anachronism these days, run for the villagers by the villagers. Which is what the original benefactors had intended it to be.

She suddenly became aware that she'd been standing outside her door, thinking tear-jerking thoughts, for minutes rather than moments. She glanced around guiltily. Reception was empty. Only Marge was at the desk, and she was busy on the phone.

Calling herself all sorts of a fool, Nan let herself into her office. There was a mountain of mail waiting for her, but she could see at a glance that it was largely made up of Christmas cards for the patients. She would deliver them when she did her round. It was a routine that paid dividends and enabled her to see everyone each day. The night report gave her facts—seeing each patient, that fleshed out the picture.

Observation and attention to detail, an old tutor had once told her.

She crossed to the window and looked out over the

car park in front of the hospital and the field beyond, which had once been a croquet lawn in the days when the hospital had been a private house. Snow had started to fall yesterday evening and had continued throughout the night. It lay thick and crisp and even, like icing on a cake, except where Tom had evidently tried to clear it near the main entrance where the ambulance drew up, but there was still a thin layer of packed snow which had resisted his spade.

The temperature had fallen dramatically since early morning and already a thin layer of ice had formed on top of the snow. Now the lightly falling flakes were beginning to settle on the ice-hard surface.

Just as well, thought Nan. Snow was less dangerous than a sheet of ice. Tom had better not clear it again, but let nature do the job when it thawed.

Nan peered upwards. The sky was leaden. A thaw wasn't about to happen for a while yet. Rather guiltily she hoped it wouldn't. There was something about snow and Christmas that went with mince pies and carols... She grinned, she was off again.

The village oldies had been shaking their heads ominously for days. 'Mark my words, Matron, there's a lot up there,' they'd said, almost in unison, when she'd been doing her round yesterday morning. 'We're in for a packet this year, like in 'ninety-one—or was it 'ninety-two?'

Actually, Nan wanted to say, it was nineteen-ninety, when Aunt Janet nearly died and I came down to Tintore to nurse her and stayed to lick my own wounds. It snowed that winter. She suppressed a sigh. Had it really been ten years ago?

'But it was worse in 'eighty-seven—though even

that wasn't as bad as 'seventy-five.' The elderly patients in the sitting room continued to argue affably.

Nan smiled and left them to it—village history was their province. They were great characters, these village elders, men and women she'd become very fond of over the years. They were tough, too. It wasn't surprising. The men had mostly been fishermen or sheep farmers, battling against the elements, and many of the women had worked in the fish-canning factory or the smokehouse. Long hours and hard, dirty work. The factories had closed when the fish quotas had dropped a few years ago.

Now they stood empty above the old quay on the eastern outskirts of the village, monuments to a once thriving industry. They were on the opposite hill to the hospital, their stark outlines softened by the snow, hiding a multitude of architectural sins. With their tall chimneys they might almost have been medieval castles, with the rugged Cornish village nestling at their feet.

Nan smiled at her thoughts and recalled her father saying, 'You've too much imagination, dear girl, head in the clouds. You'll have to learn be more practical and down to earth.'

Well, she'd learned to be practical and down to earth by becoming a nurse, and loved every minute of it, but it wasn't surprising that just occasionally the romantic little girl still in her burst out. No wonder her feelings about the snow were mixed.

As Matron of Tintore Cottage Hospital, she was well aware of the problems it might bring, but the idea of a white Christmas excited her as it had done when she'd been a child. She'd grown up in the north in the border country, where white Christmases were the norm.

You silly great big kid, she admonished herself. Grow up, you need your head examined. Stop romancing about snowball fights and sledging and building snowmen. All we need is a spate of broken arms and legs and a pneumonia case or two and we'll run out of beds. So get real, Winters, and start praying for our usual mild Cornish weather to return.

There was a clanking sound from outside as a car turned into the car park. Hugh Latimer had arrived. He was always the first to put chains round his tyres when the weather was suspect. This year they'd gone on when snow had first been forecast. Sensible, considering the visits he made to outlying farms straddling the steep hillsides surrounding Tintore.

Hugh was a dedicated GP, and being cautious was typical of him, Nan thought with affection. Being slow, sure and a patient listener was what made him a good doctor in this village context, but whether he would last long in today's high-tech hustle in a big city hospital was doubtful.

'But, then, neither would I after all these years,' she muttered, watching as he manoeuvred his sturdy Range Rover close to the front entrance.

Nan glanced at the old-fashioned wall clock as the hands reached ten. Dear old Hugh—not that he was that old, he was only in his fifties—always on time whatever the weather. She turned back to her desk to pick up the pile of files he would need on his round, and stood stock still for a moment. The room was warm, but she found herself shivering and her spine tingling.

'Someone walking over your grave,' Aunt Janet would have said.

Nan grinned. Aunt Janet had a proverb for every occasion.

She was reaching out to collect the files when a sudden bellow of pain and rage shattered the snow-muffled silence.

Surprise for a moment glued her to the spot. Then she was back at the window, looking out at Hugh lying huddled beside his car, an inert bundle.

'Oh, no, I don't believe it.' For an instant she froze again, then her adrenalin began to pump and she sprang into action.

'Dr Latimer's had a fall. Fetch Tom and a wheelchair and whoever you can find to help,' she ordered Marjory, as she raced through the hall. 'And contact Dr Horton. And tell Tom to bring blankets,' she called as she reached the door.

She didn't stop to see if her words had registered but flung open the wide front door, sped through the porch and crouched down beside the prone figure of the doctor.

'Hugh, open your eyes, talk to me.' She tore off her cardigan and draped it round his head. She would have liked to have made a pillow of it, but didn't dare move his head in case there was neck or spinal damage. It didn't seem likely, but she couldn't take a chance. The fluttering snow was thickening, settling on his pale face. She brushed it off and blew her warm breath on his cheeks and forehead, while massaging them gently with her fingertips. She took his temporal pulse. It was fast and weak...a bleed somewhere?

His eyes flickered open, closed and opened again.

His mouth was clamped into a thin line and pain clouded his eyes. 'Leg,' he forced out. 'Knee.'

His legs were hidden by his long padded coat of some waxed material, which was his hallmark in bad weather. She unbuttoned the lower buttons and turned it back. Injured knees could be nasty, but she wasn't prepared for the sight that met her when she exposed his leg.

She suppressed a gasp. She had expected bruising, swelling, even a dislocation—but not this. The trouser leg was torn open and the knee joint was a mess. The top of his fibula had splintered and spikes of bone were sticking through a further jagged tear in his trouser leg which was sticky with blood oozing from the partly concealed wound.

'Busted?' gasped Hugh. He was pale, and there was a bluish tinge round his mouth.

Nan nodded. 'Open fracture of fib, and patella looks shattered. Keep still, Hugh. We'll soon have you inside.' She continued to rub his cheeks to bring some warmth to them.

It was only minutes, but it seemed an age before Tom appeared, accompanied by Pat, an auxiliary nurse, and Cathy, one of the cleaners.

'Dr Latimer has broken his right leg,' she said briskly, pulling blankets from the bundle Pat was holding and draping them over Hugh. 'We must move him into the wheelchair without injuring it further. Cathy, fetch towels, please, from the linen cupboard.'

Cathy looked puzzled but didn't hesitate or ask why, just dashed back into Reception.

'Tom, you lift the doctor under his arms and take the weight of his trunk. Pat and I will support his legs. You support his good leg, Pat, with one hand,

and slide the other beneath his hips. I'll take the injured leg.' She smiled at Hugh. 'We'll be as gentle as we can, Hugh.' She caught Tom's eye and then Pat's. 'Ready?' They both nodded. 'Now, we've got to do this together...one, two, three.'

Hugh gritted his teeth and muttered an expletive under his breath as they lifted him into the wheelchair. He looked as if he might faint. It would have been safer not to have moved him, risking further damage, but on account of the weather it was a risk which had had to be taken.

Nan dared not take her hands away from supporting the broken leg, but told Pat to lower his good leg and put his foot on the footrest. 'And, Tom, let's get inside as fast as we can.'

With Nan in a semi-crouching position as she continued to take the weight of Hugh's badly injured limb, Tom backed into the porch, gently tilting the chair up the shallow step into the reception hall.

Cathy, carrying a pile of towels, met them just inside the door.

'Pat, make a pad of a towel and hand it to me—I want it to help support the knee joint. And make another pad and place it lightly over the wound. But don't press,' she instructed. 'We'll cut his trousers away presently when we get to the clinic room. Meanwhile, we'll cover the wound as best we can to keep it clean and absorb the blood. Put another pad on top of this one if it gets soaked.'

Cathy shuddered and turned away and even Tom looked a bit green.

'Let's get the doctor into the clinic room,' Nan said steadily.

Tom turned off into the corridor leading to the day

unit and Nan, still crouching, continued rather breathlessly, 'Pat, you fetch padded splints and an extension board from the store cupboard. Cathy, tell Marjory to ring Emergency Services—Dr Latimer will have to go to Truro to the orthopaedic unit. Tell them it's urgent. The doctor has a compound open fracture of the patella and fibula. Have you got that, Cathy?'

Cathy nodded and hurried back to Reception.

Hugh's eyes flickered open. He was pale and clammy. He whispered, 'Is it a bad one, Nan? It hurts like the devil.'

There was no point in trying to deceive him. 'Pretty bad, Hugh. As well as the fractured fib, there may be involvement of the tibia—a fracture beneath the head. You're bleeding slowly but profusely. I've sent for James Horton, and as soon as he gets here he'll give you a shot of morphine to make you more comfortable until we can get you shipped out.'

She mustered up a smile. They both knew that it wasn't as simple as that. It wasn't just a question of containing the external bleeding and dealing with the pain. The longer the splintered bones remained exposed, the more likely it was they would become infected and bleeding would continue to leak internally into the surrounding tissues. Added to that was the shock factor, which was high.

Hugh would know all that, but he was a patient at this moment and it was her job to reassure him.

She was panting with effort and being doubled up, but tried to sound calm and professional. 'Meanwhile, we're going to support your leg on an extension board, padded beneath the knee, and immobilise it as best we can with padded splints on either side.'

She managed another smile. 'Real textbook stuff,

and I'll have to cut away your trouser leg to apply a sterile pad over the open wound. It would be better to have you on a stretcher, but I hesitate to move you again. They'll have to do it anyway when you're transferred to the ambulance.'

'Couldn't stand another move just yet.' Hugh mumbled, and closed his eyes. 'Just get on with it,' he muttered. 'And I need fluids. You should set up a drip if the ambulance doesn't come soon.'

'I'll do that,' Nan promised.

Moments later, Pat arrived with the extension board and splints. Working in unison, with Tom again taking the weight of Hugh's torso and Nan supporting the leg, Pat slid the board under the injured limb and buttock, resting it on the seat of the wheelchair.

Nan was at last able to stand up and stretch her aching back.

'Well done,' she said to her two assistants. 'We make a good team.' She looked at Hugh and took his pulse again—faster and fainter. Which was the priority—drip or splints? Splints. She must immobilise the leg and try to stem the bleeding. She could fill him up with fluids when that was done.

Dr Horton arrived as she was about to fix the side splints. He had long since retired from regular practice, but occasionally helped Hugh out. Nan put him quickly in the picture and told him what she planned to do.

'All you can do,' he agreed.

He had a few words with Hugh and gave him a shot of morphine. Then whilst Nan, with help from Pat and Tom, cut away Hugh's trouser leg and fixed the side splints in position, he put up a glucose and saline drip to replace lost fluids.

In an aside he murmured to Nan, 'If we can't get him to Truro soon, we'll have to get some blood into him. Do you know his group?'

'Yes, fortunately, it's O and we've got a few bags in the fridge. How long do you think we can wait?'

'A couple of hours at a guess, but without a test to see what his haemoglobin levels are...' The old doctor shrugged.

Hurrying and breathless, Marjory came through from Reception. 'I've got Emergency Services on the line—they want a word. They're sending the air ambulance as they can't get through by road, and the lifeboat's out on another call. They want more info about...' she hesitated and glanced at Dr Latimer, now almost asleep after the injection of morphine '...the doctor.'

'Right, I can come now. While I'm talking to them, will you get through on the other line to the medical agency in Truro and find out if they've got a general practitioner who could do an emergency locum over the next few days?'

Marjory gaped at her. 'What, over Christmas? You've got to be joking.'

Nan shook her head. 'Nope, deadly serious. Just try.'

She spoke to the air ambulance medical officer, Robin Baker, told him exactly what the position was and gave him the patient's name. That it was Hugh Latimer, another medico, opened doors as if by magic. They would send a doctor with the helicopter to watch the bleed and control the drip.

The biggest bonus of all—when Nan asked him if they would bring in a locum if she was lucky enough to get one, he offered the services of a well-qualified

GP and surgeon, who was joining the air ambulance service some time in the next year. 'He's at a loose end at the moment, just come back from Australia. He doesn't seem to have family or a base here and is putting up in a hotel,' explained Robin. 'He seems to be raring to go. He's UK-registered so there's no problem there. Any good to you?'

'God bless you, Robin,' Nan said with feeling. 'You've made my day—what's more, you've made my Christmas. Things are getting a bit frantic on the preparation front and I'm needed all over the place.'

'That's because you run a home from home there,' said Robin, chuckling, 'rather than a hospital. Don't know what your new locum will think of it...'

There was suddenly a lot of buzzing and static on the line, and then it went silent.

Nan shrugged. 'Mine's gone dead.'

'Mine, too,' said Marjory in disgust, slamming the receiver down. She looked at Nan. 'Gone, *finito*. I bet the lines are down, though the whole village might not be affected. Not that I was having any joy with the agency. It looks as if we're stuck, apart from the help that dear old Doc Horton can give. And I don't want to add to your problems, but I don't think he's looking very well.'

Nan pulled a face. 'Oh, no, the poor old thing. I was so concerned about Hugh I didn't notice. I'll go and take over from him. Not that there's a lot more we can do for Hugh. It's going to take some fancy orthopaedic work to get his leg back together. But don't worry about the agency, Marge. Robin has come to the rescue, in more ways than one. He's sending us a locum when they pick up Hugh.'

'Oh, that's brilliant. Any idea who?'

'Nope, but he can use a stethoscope and is qualified to sign a prescription. What more do we need? Oh, and give Aunt Janet a buzz on the mobile—hope she's got hers switched on—and let her know what's happening. Tell her to get the spare room ready. Our locum's going to need a bed for a few nights.'

Nan returned to the day unit. Hugh was in a morphine-induced doze and looked reasonably comfortable. Pat had arranged a pillow behind his head and had started a quarter-hourly chart, noting temperature, pulse, respirations and blood pressure.

'Well done,' Nan praised, thinking proudly that *her* auxiliaries were well trained and didn't need everything spelled out for them. She checked the drip and adjusted it slightly.

Old Dr Horton was sitting on a chair, leaning back against a wall. His eyes were closed and he looked exhausted, his face drawn and more lined than usual.

Nan touched his hand. 'Dr Horton,' she said softly.

He jerked up and frowned at her. 'Where the devil…? Oh, yes, Hugh.' He started to struggle up.

Nan pushed him gently back against the wall. She was quite alarmed by the greyness of his face and his shallow breathing. 'Hugh's comfortable,' she assured him. 'And the air ambulance is coming to collect him in the next hour or so. They're also bringing in a locum to cover for a few days, so you can go home and rest. Have a hot toddy and let your wife spoil you rotten.'

The old doctor raised a smile. He stood up. 'She'll like that,' he said. 'And so will I. You're sure…?' He nodded toward Hugh.

'Positive. Now go before I get Tom to chuck you out—that's if you think you can manage to drive.'

Dr Horton snorted. 'The day I can't drive,' he said, wagging a finger, 'will be when I'm in my box on the way to the churchyard.'

Nan kissed his cheek. 'You're what Aunt Janet calls an ornery old fool,' she said. 'But we love you for it. See you and Mrs H for the carol-singing on Christmas Eve.'

'Wouldn't miss it for the world,' he said.

They were prophetic words Nan would remember later.

There was nothing more anyone could do for Hugh until the air ambulance arrived. Nan sat beside him and held his hand. Robin had promised to phone in his ETA about a quarter of an hour before he was due. But with the phones down... She made an educated guess at it. They should arrive in about forty-five minutes. Presumably they would land on the lawn as they had in the past. It was the flattest piece of land around. Unless the weather worsened and they couldn't land. She wouldn't think about that. They had about half an hour to get things ready at this end.

Her brain went into overdrive as she planned the next moves. Hugh must have the minimum wait out in the freezing weather, but they must be ready and waiting for the helicopter. Normally it took only a couple of minutes to get across the car park to the field a few hundred yards away, but they'd better allow a bit longer today so that they could take it slowly over the snow.

Someone would have to inform Hugh's housekeeper, Mrs Percy, about the accident and collect some nightclothes and shaving gear for him. She sent Cathy. Tom she sent to fetch the adapted minibus-ambulance, with the raised roof and hydraulic lift to accommodate wheelchairs. Hugh would stay in the wheelchair till they transferred him to the emergency stretcher and he was hauled up into the helicopter. It was only few hundred yards, but too far to push the wheelchair in the snow.

'Leave in three side seats,' she suggested to Tom. 'There'll only be Pat and an orderly going over with us to help unload Dr Latimer, but the new doctor will need a seat coming back.'

She'd been jokingly dismissive of the locum to Marjory, but there were moments in the next half-hour when she wondered what sort of man they might expect. Was he a high-tech whiz kid or a laid-back, easygoing GP? Would he want to take over *her* hospital, or be content to let things tick along as they normally did? Had he been working in the Outback in Australia or in a city?

Sister Joyce Slater, the assistant matron, and the late morning shift of auxiliary nurses came on duty just as Nan and the others were preparing to leave for the landing area.

Nan gave Joyce a brief outline of events and left Marjory to fill in the blanks. Transferring Hugh to the bus was an exhausting business, requiring strength and ingenuity to accommodate the extension board, but Tom and Dave, the orderly who was built like a tree trunk, managed it with a minimum of fuss. Nan climbed in and sat by Hugh, holding his hand for the short journey to the field, where in the summer they held their fête.

It was freezing on the field. The freshly falling snow was settling fast. They had been there a few minutes when the buzz of helicopter engines thrummed in the distance.

If getting Hugh into the bus had been difficult, it was as nothing compared to getting him out of the wheelchair and onto the stretcher that had been lowered from the helicopter. A wind began to pick up as Robin landed and he yelled that he would have to keep the engines on. The whirling blades and the wind stirred the snow up into a storm, almost blinding them.

Everyone pulled their hoods lower and worked with bent heads as they moved Hugh from the bus lift to the ground. He could hardly be seen under a mound of blankets and plastic sheeting. Nan struggled to hold it in place as the downdraught and the wind increased.

The locum—they presumed it was the locum—a large man, bundled in a red hooded skisuit and goggles, hugging a canvas holdall, slid down the steps and turned to haul the stretcher down behind him.

He bent double as he crossed the space between the air ambulance and the wheelchair. He was followed a moment later by another man who seemed to know what he was about, probably the doctor who'd been promised. Even with help from the new arrivals, communicating with shouts and gestures, it took a huge effort to get Hugh transferred to the stretcher and then into the helicopter.

Nan kissed his cheek and murmured a few words of comfort before he was whisked up into the interior of the machine and the steps were hauled in behind him.

Robin waved, the 'copter rose, slowly at first and then faster, until it wheeled round and sped off in the general direction of Truro, leaving another miniature snowstorm behind.

In spite of the wind and the swirling snow, by comparison it was almost silent after it had gone.

Nan watched until it was a dot in the distance, her heart going with Hugh. If only she could have gone with him—he needed a friend.

Tom said gruffly, 'Shall we be off, then, Matron? The others are in the bus.'

Nan pulled herself together. She still had a hospital to run and people to take care of, and she hadn't even said hello to the locum.

'Yes, of course, Tom.' She walked across to the minibus. Through the misted-up windows she could see the blurred shapes of Pat and Dave, and next to them the new doctor. 'I meant the new man to sit in the front, Tom,' she said, but the words were torn away in a sudden gust of wind and thickening snow.

Tom shrugged and opened the passenger door. She didn't know whether he hadn't heard or didn't care. He obviously wanted to get into the warmth as soon as possible—he wasn't interested in protocol.

She slid into her seat and half turned to look over her shoulder before she fastened her seat belt. It was dim in the bus and her hood obscured the passengers in the back seats. She pushed the hood aside. 'Hi,' she said over her shoulder, lifting her hand in salute. 'Welcome to Tintore Cottage Hospital, Doctor...'

'Mackintosh,' said a voice, 'Callum Mackintosh.' A large hand reached out and clasped hers. 'Hello, Nan, long time no see.'

CHAPTER TWO

I WON'T faint, Nan told herself, struggling to take a breath. Her heart and lungs felt as if every ounce of blood and air were being sucked out of them.

'Hello, Nan, long time no see.' She repeated the words in her head. Had she imagined them? No! It had been Callum's voice, as gravelly and distinctive now as it had been all those years ago. The rich Scottish burr was there. What was it they used to say at St Maggie's? 'Sean Connery, eat your heart out.'

Her fingers were being squeezed. How long had she been sitting there, uncomfortably twisting round, with *his* gloved hand holding hers over her shoulder? She tugged her hand free and twisted round to face the front. But removing her hand from his did nothing to stop her heart threatening to leap out of her chest like a wild thing.

The bus was moving. There was talking and laughing in the back. Had they noticed anything? They stopped. They were at the front entrance. Pat and Dave were piling out and Tom was looking at her, saying something from a long way off about Hugh's car...

'Shall I put Doc Latimer's car under cover? He's not going to be needing it for a while, is he? I'll take it back to his place when this lot eases off.' He waved a hand at the blizzard outside.

'Good idea, Tom, you do that. And tell Mrs Percy that we'll keep her informed about how the doctor's doing.' Her voice sounded normal—amazing, not a squeak in it—yet she could have sworn that her tongue was stuck to the roof of her mouth and her lips hadn't moved. Funny, she couldn't seem to move anything else either. Her feet seemed to be locked to the floor and her hands heavy on her lap.

Tom was saying something again, his voice strange and still far-away. 'Will do. I'll put it away right now, but I'll leave the bus here. I reckon I'm going to be needing it later—there'll be a few people to run home.' He glanced at Callum in the back seat. 'See you around, Doc.'

'See you, Tom,' said Callum, raising his hand.

Tom got out and closed the door quickly. Even so, a few flakes of snow swirled in. Faintly he could be heard crunching away over the snow... and then there was silence within the bus, though the wind raged outside.

Moments—or possibly minutes—later, Callum heaved a huge theatrical sigh. 'So, we're alone at last, Nannette.' The low gravelly voice was mocking, sexy.

Only *he* ever dared call her Nannette, knowing that she'd had an intense dislike of her baptismal name. Even her elderly parents, who'd given it to her, only ever called her Nan.

'It's too fluffy, too soft—it's not just *me*,' she'd said when official letters had come addressed to 'Miss Nannette Winters'. She'd added darkly, 'Whoever heard of a career-woman called Nannette? It's like something out of a musical—ridiculous. I won't be taken seriously with a name like that.'

She'd given a snort of derision. 'It's bad enough having to convince the powers that be that being short and blonde doesn't mean brainless, without having a silly name.' And she'd tilted her neat rounded chin upwards, lifted her head, crowned with its thick beautifully designer-cut tawny blonde hair, and stretched herself to her full height of five feet two.

Usually Callum had said something reassuring about size not being everything and pointed out that she'd already proved that she'd got brains. She'd been a super nurse, brilliant, with two qualifications and more to go for.

Occasionally, though, he'd teased her about her antipathy to her name. He'd always apologised, excusing it by saying, 'I like to see you angry, see your feathers ruffled. I know it's corny to say you look beautiful when you're all riled up, but you are, Nan. You're a small, neat little pouter pigeon, and I love you.' It had always ended in kissing and cuddling and sexy love-making.

That had been then, but how could he now mock her, make fun of the situation? Wasn't he in the least bit shaken by this meeting out of the blue? What they had once had together, didn't it mean anything to him? Nan stared straight ahead, as still as a statue, watching the snow being driven almost horizontally before the gusting wind.

The whirling flakes were lit up by the external lights round the entrance. It was almost dark, although it was only early afternoon. The lights had come on automatically.

Was it only early afternoon? She seemed to have lost track of time. She could see the snow, hear the wind howling, yet she felt cut off from the outside world.

Callum's voice came from behind her head. 'So

this is the famous Tintore Cottage Hospital. Word has it that it's small but beautiful. A model of what a cottage hospital should be, run by a small but beautiful dragon disguised as Matron.'

The here and now suddenly switched back on, and she came down to earth with a bang. Adrenalin and endorphins cut in. What was she doing, sitting here, mesmerized by a voice from years ago, when she had work to do? Nan scrabbled to unfasten her seat belt. Damn, angry that she was, she was all fingers and thumbs.

'Want any help?' asked Callum, gently, solicitously.

She ground her teeth and found what she hoped was her usual voice. 'No, thanks,' she replied curtly as her seat belt opened with a click. Gathering her courage, she turned round and faced him. It was dim in the bus and she still couldn't see his face very well.

Not that she needed to. She knew that there was a network of lines at the corners of his eyes that crinkled up when he laughed—and he laughed a lot, or had done in the old days. She knew that there were other lines, too, deep horizontal ones across his forehead when he frowned or raised his eyebrows, and lines appeared beside his mouth when he was tired after hours on duty, or when he was particularly worried about a patient.

She knew that if she took off her glove and ran her fingers round his jawline, she would feel the silky growth of his afternoon beard, pale blond and glossy like his hair... *Stop*!

'What are you doing here, Callum?' That was pretty cool, firm and unruffled, although in her head her voice sounded tinny and uncertain.

He answered cheerfully, the well-remembered hint

of laughter there in his voice, as it always had been when he'd teased her. 'Making myself useful, I hope. I was under the impression that you needed a locum, and I need a job for a week or so. It seems that our needs coincide. I'm heaven-sent, you might say. Not gift-wrapped, but an early Christmas present.' The gravelly tone dropped a notch. 'I thought you might be pleased to see me Nan. Are you?'

There was no apology, no pain reflected in his voice. He was being his usual breezy, arrogant self. Ten years on and he hadn't changed. There might be the odd thread or two of grey hair—it was impossible to see in the dim light—but basically he hadn't changed. Clearly he hadn't grieved as she'd grieved when they'd parted.

She could just see his smile. That wide smile that tilted the corners of his mouth. The smile that had reassured a thousand patients and had done extraordinary things to her heart—and the heart of any female within a five-mile radius. She groaned.

He leaned forward till his face was almost touching hers. Now she could see the laughing hazel eyes. 'What's wrong, Nan?' The deep voice was deeper, the burr more pronounced.

She took several deep breaths. If he could play games—if he *was* playing games—pretending that the past hadn't happened, hadn't left its mark, so could she. He wasn't going to rock her boat, destroy all her work of the last ten years. She was immune to him, had to be. That's what vaccination was for—to immunise—and she'd been well and truly vaccinated against the love bug.

Long ago she'd had a bad dose of being in love with Callum Mackintosh and, like an infectious disease, one severe bout of infection had immunised her for life. It was up to her to make him see that the vaccination had worked and would continue to work. Just as a one-off inoculation in the past against smallpox generally immunised for ever.

She was brisk and blunt. 'You're wrong, Callum—you. You don't fit in here in our little hospital. I've got unattached and some attached females on my staff who just might fall for your brand of charm, so don't go spreading it around.' She summoned up a light laugh and wagged a finger at him. 'I'm warning you, Dr Mackintosh, don't you dare upset my Christmas or New Year rosters. They're set in cement. The smooth running of my hospital depends on everyone sticking to them.'

That was telling him, she thought pettishly, letting him know that it was her nurses and the hospital she was concerned for, not herself. She blushed at her childishness. How could she let him affect her and cause her to behave so out of character? She must get a grip on herself. Convince him that just as he'd evidently made a good and complete recovery from what had ailed them in the dim and distant past so had she.

There were no after-effects. They could be good friends, surely. After all, it was Christmas—goodwill and all that. Perhaps his teasing style was what was needed. OK, she was willing to go along with that. They would have to put on a good face for the benefit of the patients and staff and, of course, Aunt Janet.

Most of all for Aunt Janet. She was the only person in Tintore who knew the whole truth—well, almost the whole truth—about herself and Callum. How would she react to Callum's sudden arrival in the village? Would she buy the 'just good friends' story?

Enough speculating. Nan made herself look directly into Callum's eyes. He was so close that she could feel his warm breath fanning her cheeks, smell his soap. He was still using musk, sensual and sexy.

He said softly, emotion thickening his throaty burr, 'Nan, I wouldn't do anything to upset your rosters or upset you. You'd better believe me. I'm not the man I was. I've changed.'

Really! thought Nan. In what way changed?

'I've come here to work, to help out. When I learned your name, realised who I was going to be working with, I was bowled over, shattered. I wondered if I could possibly do it, work with you day after day... I gave Robin the third degree, trying to find out all that I could about you and about the hospital. According to him, you've got a unique place here and it's all down to you.'

'Aunt Janet was a good act to follow.'

There was a small silence, then he said in a strained voice, 'Is she...? Did she...?'

'Survive?'

'Yep.'

He sat back on the side seat and Nan felt safer with some space between them, though the space did nothing to still her trembling heartbeats. And the familiar scent of him still clung, assaulted her senses, made her feel vulnerable, helpless. She was a breath or two away from throwing herself into his arms.

Again she reminded herself that she was the matron of a small but efficient hospital, a woman with responsibilities.

Focus on what he'd just said. Did his hesitant questioning mean that he felt some guilt after all for his attitude to Aunt Janet's illness ten years ago? Would he react differently if the same thing happened now? She doubted it. He was a career medic through and through...though if that were true what was he doing here, acting as locum to a small-town GP? It didn't add up.

She breathed in very deeply.

'Yes, Janet survived. She's seventy-something now, still does the odd covering stint for me if required. She's tough, came through the marrow transplant and the chemotherapy with flying colours. But it took time before she was properly back on her feet, too late for her to take over again as matron.'

'So you stayed on.' There was awe in his voice as he said it. 'All these years. How could you do it, Nan, ditch your career plan like that?' What had happened to his career plan?

'Easily.' That wasn't true. It had been hell in the beginning, for the first two or three years, in fact.

'I don't believe you, Nan,' Callum said softly. 'I know you too well. At twenty-five you had two good qualifications under your belt and were all set to get another. You were heading for the top job in the top hospital. You wouldn't give up your career plan for me...remember?'

Of course she remembered. It had been the final crack—chasm—in their relationship.

'Past history,' Nan snapped. 'I grew up, fast. I was very naïve in those days. It was a greedy time, still is out there.' She waved her hand at the snowed-up windows. 'Everyone wanted—still wants—power and money. I felt that I had to compete with my peers. I kidded myself that by getting to the top I could alter the way nursing was going.'

She paused and added with a dry chuckle, 'But it wouldn't have happened, Callum, even if I had got to the top. It took me a while to realise it, but I'm a hands-on nurse with organising ability, nothing more. I'd have been a complete dud at managing a huge techno-orientated hospital in London or anywhere else. I'm happy here at Tintore Cottage Hospital. In our own small way we do our bit—the village needs us. This is my life.'

Callum had almost held his breath while Nan was talking, afraid to interrupt and break the flow. He felt he was learning more about her at this moment than he'd learned in the past when they'd worked, lived and made love together. Now he leaned forward and touched her cheek with his gloved fingers. Even through his gloves he felt her tremble and marvelled at it. Did he really have the power to make her tremble?

Nan hesitated for a moment, then placed her hand over his and let her gaze meld with his, and she actually found herself chuckling. All the old magic was there between them in the depths of his laughing eyes, just as there had been in the old days when they'd been so much in love. Though it had been a love that they hadn't acknowledged as such—they'd called it anything but love.

But whatever it was, the magic and the laughing had disappeared in those last few days. They'd suddenly grown dark and hard.

Yet they were laughing again now.

So what had turned the laughter back on within minutes of them coming together again? Callum, of course. That was his speciality, turning tears into laughter, and the years hadn't changed that, though he'd said that he'd changed.

What had he been doing all these years that had changed him? And what was he doing as a medic with the Cornwall-based air ambulance service? Had he ditched all his plans to become the world's most renowned anaesthetist? He was to have discovered new combinations of drugs with fewer and fewer side-effects to make long, tricky operations successful—and certainly the operations were getting longer and trickier.

That had been his ambition once upon a time, that was why he'd been head-hunted by a huge American pharmaceutical company. So what had happened that had been powerful enough to end his dreams when their love, or whatever it had been, and her need of him hadn't been strong enough to even slow him down? The questions raged as they sat in the dim quiet sanctuary of the bus.

On a breathy sigh, she whispered, 'Oh, Callum, why have you come back into my life?'

'I didn't come seeking you out, Nan, although when fate brought me to Cornwall...' He cupped his other hand round her chin. 'I didn't expect to find you here after ten years, but I hoped to get news of you, perhaps track you down. I never in a million years dreamed that I would meet up with you within days of arriving here. When Robin mentioned Tintore and said that they needed a locum at the hospital, I came as near to passing out as I ever have done, and I jumped at the chance.'

Nan's heartbeats were still going like the clappers

as he spoke. She'd never expected to hear his voice again, and yet here he was a few feet away from her.

'You said that fate brought you here—what fate?' There was some substance in her voice now.

'It's a long story, love, ironic, considering the way we parted. I want to tell all, Nan, but not now—later. Perhaps we can retrieve something from our past.' He kissed her tenderly on her mouth before she could draw back.

Retrieve something from their past! Was it possible? Did she want it? Slowly Nan gathered herself together and eased his hands from her face. With the tip of her tongue she traced the outline of her lips. She could still feel the pressure of his mouth on hers. It was as it had been before—hours after he'd kissed her, she'd always been able to feel the imprint on her mouth.

Don't think about it, she warned herself. Come down to earth.

She said briskly, 'As you say, Callum, now isn't the time.' She glanced at the clock on the dashboard. 'I don't believe it—it's nearly three o'clock. God knows what sort of story my lot are cooking up in there. I dare say word's already about that you and I are old...*friends*, unless you told them otherwise?'

Callum shook his head. 'Scout's honour, I didn't breathe a word,' he said drily, 'but I guess this is like any hospital and tongues wag.'

'Our intelligence service is second to none,' Nan replied with equal dryness. 'There'll be a reception committee waiting for us when we go in. Everyone will want to give you the once-over. You're going to cause quite a stir.'

'Oh,' he said, his voice sounding meek. 'I hope I pass muster as an old *friend*.'

'Huh,' replied Nan sceptically as she climbed out of the bus. 'I dare say you'll get by.'

Of course he would get by. Callum always did. Amongst his attributes was his ability to make friends easily with men or women. They fell like ninepins before his charm, his charisma. Ruthlessly she squashed thoughts of how readily she had fallen to those charms. She must concentrate on the here and now, she reminded herself grimly.

Nan was terribly conscious of him beside her as, heads down against the driving snow, they made a dash for the porticoed front door.

Marjory was still behind the reception desk where she'd been since the crack of dawn, which seemed a lifetime ago. Pat, Dave, Joyce and Polly Bowen, a trained nursery nurse, were at the desk, too. They all turned expectant faces toward the door as Nan and Callum, accompanied by a gust of wind and snow, virtually blew into the hall.

Nan forced a grin. 'I said there'd be a reception committee, didn't I?' she mouthed at Callum.

There was a flurry of activity from the group round the desk, as if they were all meant to be there, but they couldn't keep the curiosity out of their faces.

Callum smiled at everyone and Nan could practically hear four female hearts ricocheting against ribs. The magic hadn't diminished one iota.

Nan took a deep breath and moved toward the desk. Now for the tricky bit—introductions without giving herself away, especially to Marge with her X-ray eyes. Keep it simple but try to inject a little humour.

'I'm sure the bush telegraph's already been busy,'

she said, grinning at Pat and Dave, 'and you all know that this is Dr Callum Mackintosh. He has nobly come to our aid, even though it is Christmas, and I'm sure he would rather be with his family. So I want you to give him a warm Tintore welcome.' She tried a throw-away laugh, wondering why he wasn't with his family. 'Good Lord, I sound like a TV chat show host, don't I?'

Marge saw through her and came to her aid. Had her laugh been that nervous?

'You could get a job on the telly any day, Matron,' she said, a smile lighting up her plain face. She thrust out her hand in Callum's direction. 'Marjory Rivers, secretary - cum - receptionist - cum - general dogsbody.' Her brown eyes gleamed with wicked humour. 'As Matron instructed, welcome to Tintore and especially the hospital. We're going to keep you busy while you're here, and I don't just mean tending the sick.'

Callum took her hand and returned her smile. He shook his head. 'You've lost me,' he said.

Marge looked him up and down and put her head on one side. 'What are you—around six feet?'

'Give or take an inch either way.'

'Just right—' Marge grinned '—for putting angels on top of Christmas trees and balloons in awkward corners.' She turned to the uniformed figure beside her. 'Wouldn't you say, Joyce?'

Joyce nodded. 'Definitely,' she said. 'And he'll make a splendid Santa Claus.' She offered her hand to Callum. 'Joyce Slater, Matron's sometimes willing slave and assistant. And this...' she indicated Polly '...is Polly Bowen, one of our valued army of auxiliary nurses.'

Polly, fluttering long eyelashes, stepped forward and there was another handshake. 'Like Sister Joyce said,' she murmured, slipping into the local vernacular, 'you'm very welcome to Tintore, Dr Mackintosh.'

Nan watched with surprise and amusement as her staff went through their paces and teased Callum mercilessly. It seemed that they were they all hell bent on being comedians. It had to be because it was Christmas and they were in pantomime mode.

Heaven knew what sort of a build-up Dave and Pat had given Callum, and what they'd learned in the few minutes they'd chatted to him in the bus, but obviously it had been enough to know that he wouldn't be offended by their teasing.

Far from it, of course. He loved it, responded to it and accepted it for what it was—a welcome to make him feel one of 'the family'. He assured them that he was ready and willing to help out in almost any capacity. 'Do I really have to put on a red dressing-gown and long white beard and play Daddy Christmas?' he asked plaintively.

Nan recovered something of her usual poise. 'You do,' she said, even managing a laugh. 'That's part of your locum duties. Hugh does it every year. If you refuse...'

The telephone rang—and rang again. They all stared at it.

Callum said in a voice suddenly full of authority, 'Isn't anyone going to answer that?' He stretched out a hand, but Marge beat him to it.

'Good afternoon, this is Tintore Cottage Hospital. Can I help you?'

Nan said softly to Callum, 'The lines have been down since early this morning, which is why we were all struck dumb. Obviously they've been repaired—it usually takes them days. Thank God we're back in business *pro tem*.'

Marge put down the receiver. 'That was Jack Beecham…'

'Village policeman,' murmured Nan to Callum.

'He's bringing in old Henry Forrest—he found him lying under a hedge with his arms full of a dead sheep. Reckons he's probably been there since early this morning. He's barely conscious and very cold, and Jack thinks he might have broken his wrist or arm. He's wrapped him in car rugs. He'll be here in about fifteen minutes. Oh, and Jack says he's trying to raise old Henry's son to let him know what's happened, but hasn't had any joy yet.'

To Callum, it seemed that Nan suddenly gained in stature and became every inch a matron.

'Pat, you and Polly make up a bed in Long Stay and put in a slow-warming blanket. Pat, you stay and special Henry when he arrives—make up a quarter-hourly chart and start getting some warm drinks into him when he's conscious. And you'd better have the resuscitation trolley at the ready, just in case. Polly, when you've helped Pat with the bed, get back to the kids' ward and start them off decorating their tree as promised, or we'll have a riot on our hands.' She turned to her deputy. 'Is that all right with you, Joyce?'

'Fine.' Joyce looked at her watch. 'And Dave and Tom should stand by with a wheelchair to help Jack get the old boy out of the car.'

Nan nodded. 'Right, off you go, Dave, and make sure he's well covered up before you move him out of the car. Take care not to damage his arm—rest it on a pillow.'

'OK, Matron,' said Dave. 'Will do.'

Nan turned back to Joyce. 'I think we'd better have the mobile X-ray and a splints trolley at the ready. We may need to immobilise old Henry's arm whilst we're warming him up.'

'I'll get that sorted stat.' Joyce raised her eyes ceilingwards. 'The last thing we want is another complicated fracture that we can't deal with here.' She marched swiftly off down the corridor.

'I'll second that,' said Marge.

Joyce's words reminded Nan of the rescue flight and Callum's presence. She whirled round and found him standing a few feet behind her, a smile crooking up one side of his mouth. She was amazed that she'd forgotten he was there. It had never happened before—in the old days she'd always sensed his presence before she'd seen him. Relief flooded through her. Good, that must mean that she was really over him. Her first reaction to him in the bus had been simply because of the shock.

She smiled happily at him. 'Callum, I'm so sorry. I—'

'Don't be. I've enjoyed watching a well-ordered machine go into action.' He stepped forward and smiled down at her. 'You haven't lost your touch, Nan,' he purred. 'Everyone still jumps to your say-so.' His eyes danced. 'Haven't you got any instructions for me, Matron?'

She wasn't over him, not this close! The smell of him—the smile—the laughing eyes. She prickled all over and her legs felt numb. She managed a shaky step backwards and felt the reception desk behind her.

Relieved, she turned and said to Marge, 'While we're in business with the phone, contact Truro and find out if Dr Latimer's arrived yet. And give them our mobile number in case the phone goes off again. Tell them I want to be kept informed.' She didn't want to turn back and face Callum. 'Oh, and, Marge, phone Mrs Horton and find out if Dr Horton got home safely.'

'Right away, Matron.' Marge's eyes flicked between Nan and Callum and made lightning deductions.

Nan gave her a wry smile knowing she'd be in for a grilling later.

At that moment Tom and Dave appeared with a wheelchair and on cue, siren blasting, the police car could be heard coming up the drive.

By virtue of having four hefty men available, getting old Henry out of the car and into the wheelchair was infinitely easier than moving Hugh Latimer had been earlier. Callum not only contributed muscle but know-how.

'Why *old* Henry?' he asked as he and Nan climbed the stairs to the first floor and the long-stay wards a few minutes later, leaving the lift free for Tom, Dave and the wheelchair. 'He doesn't look that ancient— in his seventies at a guess and that's not old these days, especially for an outdoor active type, though, that said, I'm amazed that he survived several hours in this temperature.'

'He's tough, like a lot of the oldies. Age-wise, try late nineties—he's ninety-seven. As for old Henry, it's because his son is a Henry—young Henry.'

Seeing Callum's astonishment, she chuckled. 'Young Henry's only seventy. There are plenty of father-son, mother-daughter combinations in Tintore. We're a very closed community even in this day and age.' Nan grinned at him. 'Believe it or not, I'm still sometimes called the young matron to distinguish me from Aunt Janet, the old matron.'

Callum gave a muted hoot of laughter and stopped on the top stair, his hazel eyes positively sparkling. 'The *young* matron, who'd have thought it? Ten years ago...'

Nan's spine prickled and she stumbled on the top step. She shouldn't have said anything remotely connected with their past, and mentioning Aunt Janet had certainly done that. She wanted to laugh with him, but couldn't. She couldn't believe how much his laughter hurt.

Callum caught her arm. She shook it off and said in a low voice, 'I think the least said about ten years ago the better, Callum, at least until we can talk about it properly. It may be irrational, but that's how I feel. I can put on a face, but at the moment that's the best I can do.'

The laughter in Callum's eyes died. He said in a subdued voice, 'Yes, you're right. Insensitive of me. Sorry, Nan.' They were standing at the top of the stairs, with wide corridors branching away to left and right. Both corridors were empty.

Nan was already regretting her uptight reaction to his remark. She smiled up at him. 'I'm sorry, too, Callum, I think I'm still in shock from your sudden reappearance in my life. I haven't recovered my equilibrium. Shall we call a truce?' She held out her hand.

He clasped it in both his hands and raised it to his lips. 'Truce,' he murmured, 'and may it be a long, happy truce...'

Nan shivered. She felt as if she were floating somewhere between the ceiling and the floor. 'I second that,' she whispered.

Callum risked brushing a kiss across her cheek. 'Then let's go and give our patient the once-over and make him as comfortable as we can,' he said.

CHAPTER THREE

OLD Henry, drowsy, but already fully conscious, was safely tucked up in bed against a sloping mound of pillows, his arm in a simple sling supported on another pillow. Pat was with him and about to take his temperature, but stepped back from the bed with a smile when Nan and Callum appeared.

'He's opened his eyes several times,' she explained, 'but he's not really with us yet. I was going to take his axillary temperature so as not to disturb him too much.'

'Good thinking,' said Callum, 'but I'm afraid that I'll have to disturb him a little, if someone could provide me with a stethoscope—mine's somewhere at the bottom of my kit bag. I'd like to examine Mr...'

Pat handed him the stethoscope from the resuscitation trolley. 'Forrest,' she said.

'Thanks, Nurse.' Callum gave her a brilliant smile and predictably she blushed to the roots of her fair greying hair. He bent over the patient. 'Mr Forrest, my name's Callum Mackintosh. I'm a doctor and I'd like to listen to your chest to see if you've suffered any ill effects from being out in the cold for so long.'

The old man opened his eyes. They were astonishingly blue, but puzzled. 'Where's Doc Latimer?' he croaked. His eyes swivelled to Nan and relief washed over his face. He stretched out a large bony hand, which, in spite of its size and roughness, looked pathetic. Nan took it between her hands and massaged it gently.

'The doctor's in hospital, Henry. He broke his leg, slipping on the snow, like you've probably broken your arm.'

The old man grimaced. 'We'm a right pair of old fools, aren't we?'

'You could say that,' Nan answered with a smile.

'But we'm telling you,' Henry fixed his eyes on Callum, as if realising that he would have to answer to him, 'if it be broken, we'm not going into the city hospital. We'm staying here.' His mouth set in a stubborn line.

Callum nodded. 'If it is broken, Mr Forrest, there shouldn't be any need for you to go to Truro. We can fix your arm here. It looks as if you've got a clean break which hasn't broken the skin, and which we'll be able to immobilise. We'll confirm that with an X-ray after I've finished examining you.'

Joyce arrived with the mobile X-ray machine as Callum was speaking.

He bent over the bed and examined old Henry with the careful concentration that Nan remembered of old. He paid particular attention to the bony chest, palpating it gently with his fingers before using the stethoscope.

Straightening up, he smiled down at the old man. 'Well Mr Forrest, you're remarkably fit in spite of being exposed to the bitter cold for hours, though your chest is a bit wheezy. I want to keep you in for a couple days—stabilise your temperature, which is still low, and start you off on an antibiotic. Is that all right with you, sir?'

Old Henry grunted and nodded his head. He was obviously very tired.

'All finished, Doctor?' Joyce asked.

'All finished, thank you, Sister,' Callum confirmed, and stepped back to make room for her to push the X-ray machine into position. He brushed against Nan and, in an aside, muttered, 'I did a brief course in radiology so that I could cope in some of the out-of-the-way places in which I might find myself, but I'm a bit on the rusty side, though I dare say I'll cope.'

Nan, conscious of the peculiar sensation that the brief touch of his arm had triggered off, eased away from him. It was as if he were still pressing against her. Surely he couldn't really have this effect on her after all these years? For heaven's sake, she was a mature woman, not a romantic, inexperienced girl—if there was such a thing these days.

She would play it cool and amused, play on the fact that he was for once ruffled, a little unsure of himself. She arched her eyebrows and gave him a wicked, teasing smile. It was odd to hear him confessing to being nervous, and immensely reassuring to know that he had some shortcomings and wasn't squeaky clean perfect, as he had once seemed to her.

In a tongue-in-cheek voice, she said softly, 'Not to worry, Doctor. You won't have to cope. Joyce qualified as a radiographer, before taking up nursing.'

Callum visibly relaxed. 'Phew, what a relief. I might have known you would have everything organised,' he said drily. 'The efficient Matron Winters.'

A touch of sarcasm or a compliment? Nan wondered. They watched as Joyce positioned the machine and explained to Henry what she was going to do. Then, with Pat's help, she proceeded to take several pictures, moving to focus on different parts of the old man's forearm.

Callum whistled softly through his teeth. 'Don't know why you need a locum,' he grumbled, but this time his eyes were full of admiration and he definitely meant his comment as a compliment. 'You and your merry band seem pretty well self-sufficient.'

Nan, pleased to have surprised him, letting him see that though Tintore geographically might be a backwater on the care front they were second to none, said happily, 'It's a question of compromise, tapping all available resources, stretching and sometimes bending the rules. There's a lot of talent in a village like this and huge support for the hospital. We've got our own pharmacist—she owns the post office and general stores and runs the chemist section. Absolutely essential here with the next chemist miles away over the moors.

'But you will have your moment of glory, Callum. We've never had anyone yet specialising in anaesthetics, and now here you are—you're a real bonus.'

'Surely there aren't any occasions when you need an anaesthetist. You don't do surgery requiring general anaesthesia, do you?'

'Occasional emergency surgery when it's easier for an anaesthetist to come to us than to ship the patient to Truro. We're capable of nursing post-operative patients. And we have two maternity beds and have an anaesthetist laid on if an epidural is requested. We're not always snowed in or cut off by heavy rainfall and landslides. Truro and other major hospitals in the area are often chock-a-block and only too willing for us to provide beds and nursing care when we can.'

Joyce finished taking her pictures. 'I'll be off and develop these,' she said. 'Give me ten minutes or so.'

Old Henry turned out to have mid-shaft fractures of his radius and ulna but, as Callum had suspected, they were hairline breaks and still in alignment.

'Shall I go ahead and plaster it?' Joyce asked Callum.

His lip curled, his eyes danced. 'Of course. You're an experienced plaster nurse, I presume?'

Joyce chuckled. 'For my sins,' she said.

Nan and Callum left her, assisted by Pat, to her plastering, and took themselves off on a tour of the hospital.

As they were already in the long stay unit, they started there.

Acutely conscious of Callum beside her, and trying not to be, Nan led the way along the corridor. 'This was once the female geriatric ward,' she explained, waving her hand up the length of the corridor, 'and next door to it an identical male ward. We gutted it a few years ago to produce single rooms, each with a shower, loo and basin, like the room that Harry's in. Patients can bring their own furniture and televisions if they want to.'

She hoped Callum was impressed. She gave him an oblique glance as they walked down the corridor. His pale blond hair was bleached almost white, emphasising the deep bronze tan he'd acquired in Australia or some tropical country. And his face had become leaner and more distinguished over the years. No, that wasn't the word—more serene, happier, more contented, more relaxed. And his mouth had acquired a tenderness, a softness, that was new to her.

He'd always been bright and breezy, pleased with

himself and the world—well, almost always—but there had been a brittleness about him, almost a hardness, just below the surface, which had showed if he'd been angry or at odds with his consultant boss. Occasionally his laughing eyes and soft brogue had hardened and revealed this tough streak.

Callum's voice broke through her thoughts. 'So it's a sort of retirement home as well as a hospital, hence the luxury carpeting instead of clinically clean washable flooring?' he said. It was half a question, half a statement.

Was that a criticism? Unable to bear his closeness and the warmth emanating from him, and to put a stop to her unruly thoughts, Nan moved a few inches sideways, as if distancing herself from him physically would help.

Her nervousness made her breathless and a little shrill. 'State-of-the-art vacuum-cleaners do a good enough job of keeping everywhere clean, and all surfaces are wiped down each day. And the emergency unit and day surgery are tiled and not carpeted, as are our kitchens which are a model of hygiene—you can inspect them in a minute.'

She was aware that she was sounding defensive, slightly aggressive, but couldn't seem to stop herself. She couldn't bear any sort of criticism of her hospital, and from Callum Mackintosh it was pure anathema.

Callum looked up and down the corridor, assured himself that it was empty, that even the nurses' station was unattended, and in one swift movement he swivelled Nan round to face him.

His hands were gentle but firm on her shoulders. 'Oh, Nan, I'm so sorry you're lumbered with me and I'm sorry it hurts you so much.' His eyes were full of tenderness. 'I wasn't criticising, love. I've already seen and heard enough to know that your hospital is special, and you are special, too. You've created a wonderful atmosphere of loving and caring—it positively hits you as you walk in the door.'

He looked down at her and whispered, his soft Scottish burr caressing her senses, 'Can you find it in your heart, Nan, to love me a little, open the door a crack and let me in?'

Nan thought that her heart would leap out of her breast. What was he doing to her, this man who had once been the love of her life? Her eyes must have registered something like fear, for he eased the grip on her shoulders and pleaded, 'Nan, you're not scared of me, are you?'

Scared, of course she wasn't scared—not scared, meaning physically frightened. But she *was* scared of the effect he was having on her. If this could happen after only a few hours, how might he might affect her, given a few days in his company?

For how long could she go on ignoring the occasional touch of his hand, or eye-to-eye contact, which sent quivering and amazingly familiar signals up her spine, churning up memories? Once or twice she almost believed they'd never parted, that it hadn't been ten years since she'd revelled in the touch of his hands and the warmth and sexy male scent of him.

Even when they weren't touching, the vibes between them pulsated so strongly that she felt they must be apparent to other people.

He was waiting for an answer. The corridor, miraculously, remained empty. What should she say to him? How to resist him, when all she wanted to do was to melt into him, open her mouth to feel his mouth on hers, familiar and warm?

'Nan.' For the second time he pleaded. 'Don't shut me out—give me another chance. It's Christmas. There's enough love swilling around in this place to include me, isn't there?'

This was another sign of a different Callum. The old Callum would never have pleaded. It had seemed to Nan once to have been a sign of strength—but was it? It was another thought to file away to mull over later. Right now she had to give Callum an answer to his loaded question, or rather two questions. Was she afraid of him and dared she include him in her loving?

She was terribly conscious of his hands on her shoulders and her heart doing acrobatics in her chest, which was rising and falling at a rate of knots. There was no concealing that from him. Would he realise that it was his nearness that was turning her into a quivering jelly?

There were voices at the end of the corridor and two nurses appeared, making for the station.

Callum dropped his hands and moved away slightly as Nan found her voice. The expression on his face was wary, uncertain. A wave of love surged through her, a mixture of her old love and something new that she couldn't fathom. She wanted to reassure him. She felt, for the first time since she'd come face to face with him in the bus, that she was in charge.

'No, I'm not afraid of you, Callum. Certainly not physically—emotionally perhaps.' His eyes brightened. Her voice was gentle as she added, 'But I need lots of time to get to know the new man you say exists—and you need time, too, to get to know the different me.'

He started to say something, but she shook her head. 'Not here—when we meet up later. Right now we'd better get on with our tour.'

Most of the senior residents were in the sitting room, playing cards, and barely gave them a glance as they stood in the doorway.

'Special whist match in progress,' murmured Nan. 'Better not interrupt.'

'Lord, no,' said Callum. 'I get the message. My mother's whist matches were sacrosanct.'

They smiled at each other, a smile of friendship and understanding. There was no need for words. They both had their roots in small villages where these things mattered. It had been one of the first confidences they'd exchanged when they'd met in a busy London teaching hospital.

Nan found herself smiling into Callum's eyes—ten years ago. Was he remembering?

He was. It was as if she had spoken. 'They were wonderful days, Nan.' He squeezed her hand.

'We'd better get on,' Nan said breathlessly.

They whisked round the rest of the wards. There were a lot of visitors everywhere so they didn't stay long, but Callum was given a warm welcome by everyone and it was clear that word of his arrival had already spread. It was also generally known that he and Matron Winters were old friends.

They ended up in Tiddlywinks Ward, where at present there were seven children. Callum was an especially big hit with them, behaving like a big kid himself. He bent to kiss the little girls' hands as he was introduced to them one by one, making them giggle and blush as their older female counterparts often did when singled out by Dr Mackintosh.

Nothing changes, thought Nan drily. She led him toward a bed where a little girl was lying against soft pillows, looking flushed and fragile. There was a cradle over her knees, lifting the lightweight duvet clear of her limbs.

'Rheumatoid arthritis,' diagnosed Callum as they approached the bed.

Nan nodded. 'Yes, Marie's eight. It was diagnosed a couple of years ago. She's been in remission for some time, but it started up again a few days ago. Her mum's a single parent and working, so it was thought best to admit her. Hugh planned to keep her in over Christmas. Actually, it'll be doing her and Judith, her mother, a favour. Money's tight and they'll probably have a better Christmas here than at home.'

Callum stopped in his tracks. He looked at Nan with astonished eyes. 'You'd better pinch me,' he said with a laugh. 'An English hospital allowing a bed to be occupied for social rather than medical reasons. Oh, Nan, only you could pull that off.'

Nan shook her head. 'Not true,' she said, though her heart jolted at the affectionate note in his voice. 'We've a unique set up here. The fishing-fleet owners, the Hopkinsons, built a row of almshouses for the widows and families of fishermen lost at sea. They made a mint out of processing the fish over the years and could afford to be generous. When the last Hopkinson died, he left his mansion house, the almshouses and money in trust to be converted into a hospital, with the proviso that no villager was ever turned away if in need, even if they weren't ill. I suppose he was what one could call a true philanthropist.'

The skin wrinkled up at the corners of Callum's laughing eyes in the way she so well remembered.

'Thanks for the potted history of Tintore,' he said. 'It's like something out of *Alice in Wonderland*. I've been to some out-of-the-way places over the last few years, but this is something else again.'

What out-of-the-way places? Nan wondered as they moved over to Marie's bed. 'Marie, this is Dr Mac,' she said.

Callum took the child's misshapen hand gently in his and brought it to his lips. 'Hi, there,' he said. 'This looks like fun.' He stirred the box of tree baubles she was balancing on her stomach.

Marie nodded. 'Yes, I choose which one they put up. I'm going to give them this star next.' She fished out a silver star and held it up.

A skinny little boy with a sparse, bristly head of reddish hair almost snatched it from her hand.

Nan gripped the boy's arm and frowned down at him. 'Harry, you know you mustn't grab things from Marie—you'll hurt her.'

'Leukaemia and chemotherapy?' queried Callum in a low voice.

Nan nodded. 'Yes, this is Harry,' she said, keeping her hold on the boy's arm. 'Harry, this is Dr Mac. He's going to look after you for a while whilst Dr Hugh's away.'

Harry stared at Callum very hard. 'I told her you weren't an angel,' he said, 'just because it looked as if you were flying when you came out of the helicopter. Of course, we couldn't see you very well, 'cos of the snow and it was right across the field. But *she*—'

'Wendy,' interjected Nan sternly, 'not *she* in that tone of voice.' In a quick aside to Callum, 'Wendy's diabetic.'

Harry sighed. 'Well, Wendy said...' he pointed to a small girl reaching up to hook a fancy ball on the tree '...that you could be the Archangel Gabriel, 'cos he's a man.' He frowned heavily. 'But you were wearing a red suit and I thought you might be Father Christmas, but you're not.'

Callum shook his head. 'Sorry about that, but I'm sure he'll be along on Christmas Day—probably on a sledge, I would think, considering the weather.'

'Yes,' murmured Harry thoughtfully. 'If there is a Father Christmas. What do you think Dr Mac?'

For a fleeting moment Callum was caught off guard, and then he said, 'Oh, I'm sure there must be— he used to visit me when I was as young as you. I saw him once, putting things into my stocking at the foot of the bed, and I'm sure that I heard sleigh bells as he drove off.'

His face was serious and Nan knew that he was remembering an actual incident from his childhood. It was the most truthful way of reassuring the small boy.

Harry nodded. 'Yes, I thought I heard them last year, coming down from the moors,' he said solemnly.

With the exception of Marie, who was on complete bed rest, all the other six children in the ward were helping Polly decorate the Christmas tree. And even Marie's bed had been pulled nearer the tree so that she could see what was going on and take part.

There were also two visitors lending a helping hand. Nan introduced them to Callum. One of them was Wendy's mum, Lynn, a young woman in her late twenties. The other was the mother of an eight-year-old boy, Wayne, a slender, fair-haired child suffering from glandular fever. She was an older woman in her forties named Annette.

It was obvious to Nan that both women fell under Callum's spell. What was it about him that attracted both men and women? she wondered. And why was it that, however much he might have changed in some respects, his charm, charisma, or whatever it was, was still as strong as ever?

Callum met the other three children jostling around the tree. Peter, aged ten, was on crutches. He'd suffered an open fracture of his ankle and had been returned to Tintore, after having it fixed in the orthopaedic unit in Truro.

'Peter will be going home for Christmas,' explained Nan. 'His parents are sheep farmers, and not only is the terrain up there hilly but the old-fashioned farmhouse is full of stairs and uneven surfaces. It would have been lethal for him to go home until he learned to manage his crutches.'

Callum grinned and raised an eyebrow. 'Lethal,' he agreed. He was teasing but understanding now that he was getting the measure of what the cottage hospital was all about.

There were two other children for him to meet—the nine-year-old Thompson twins, Hazel and William. They were exuberant, bouncy, friendly.

'There doesn't look much wrong with either of them,' said Callum. 'Are they to be counted as two of your waifs and strays?'

'No! They're both asthmatic and had a bad dose of flu. Until yesterday we kept them segregated in a side ward. They appear to be over the flu so we've brought them into the general ward. But you're seeing them at their best—they've been pale and lethargic and it's been tricky, controlling their asthma. They're looked after by their gran. Their father's a fisherman. His wife took off when the twins were babies and old Mrs Thompson has helped look after them ever since. She really couldn't cope when they were at their worst.'

'So they'll probably spend Christmas here,' said Callum, his eyes twinkling. 'And shall I hazard a guess that Gran and Dad will call in for Christmas dinner?'

'Probably,' confirmed Nan demurely, but her green eyes were shining, and for a moment she felt incredibly close to him, thrilled that he understood what Tintore was all about.

The children drew them to the tree, and they found themselves helping to decorate the noble fir until it was smothered in an exuberant, crowded muddle of tinsel, pretty coloured balls and figures and coloured lights. To round it off, Polly sprayed it with silver frost.

Everyone wanted Callum to do the honours and fix a chubby, rosy-cheeked fairy to the top of the tree. When he'd finished, Nan switched on the lights.

'Colourful rather than artistic,' Callum said with a grin, standing back to admire their handiwork. He added softly, under the cover of hand-clapping and oohs and aahs of delight, 'What about fire and safety precautions, or is that one of the rules you bend?'

'Certainly not,' replied Nan fiercely. 'Trust you to bring in a sour note. Do you seriously think that I would juggle with my patients' lives? The tree and decorations are all fireproofed, and the wiring and lights have been checked by Neil Ford—he's our one permanent fireman.'

Callum took a step away from her and held his

hands up in mock surrender. 'Sorry, sorry, I was definitely out of order. My goodness, Nan, you're still the same little dragon of old, capable of spitting fire and brimstone from those blazing green eyes.' His voice dropped a notch, his brogue suddenly more pronounced. 'And, oh, love, I've missed you so very much over the years.' His eyes, full of warmth and passion, burned into hers.

It was as if he were touching her, holding her in his arms. Nan held her breath and tried to look away from him, but couldn't. Mutely, they stood, a couple of feet away from each other, like statues unable to move, unable to speak, deaf to the world around them, until Polly's voice broke through from across the ward.

'Matron, the children are ready to sing their carol now. Shall we start?'

Long years of training brought Nan down from cloud nine. 'Rather. Let's get cracking, kids, what's it going to be?' She was relieved to hear her voice come out loud and clear.

Each year the children chose their own tree carol, with help from parents and staff. Most years it was 'Away in a Manger', but this year they had chosen 'The Mother Mary had a Baby Boy'.

Wayne's mother, Annette, had brought her guitar and, according to Polly who specialled the children, they had been practising with her for the past few days. This was news to Nan, and she felt a thrill of pride in the young nursery nurse who had organised this on her own initiative.

The room suddenly went very quiet as the children gathered round the tree and Marie's bed, and Annette strummed a few chords by way of introduction.

The young, trembly, treble voices of the children rang out, wafting out of the doors and down the corridor. Staff and some patients from nearby wards sidled in to listen and join in the rhythmic clapping that accompanied the carol.

'That,' murmured Callum softly when the carol came to an end, 'is tear-jerking stuff. Haven't heard anything like it since I was in Jamaica a few years back.'

A few minutes later, the tea-supper trolley arrived and, after promising that they would be back the next day to help with the rest of the decorating, Nan and Callum left the ward.

'I think you've seen everywhere except the kitchens,' said Nan as they walked down the stairs. 'Would you like to go now and have a look at them? After all, I promised that you should inspect them.'

'What I want, no, need desperately,' said Callum, 'is a large, mug of tea loaded with sugar.' He leaned against the wall at the foot of the stairs, and Nan saw that he looked suddenly exhausted. There was a greyness beneath the tan that hadn't been there before.

She clapped a hand to her mouth. 'Dear God, I haven't even offered you a drink and you've been on the go for hours. Callum, I'm so sorry. Let's get to my office where I can make you tea and give you a stiff whisky while the kettle boils. That is, if whisky is still your pick-me-up?'

'Spot on,' he murmured, and a tired smile lit up his face. 'I'm glad you remembered.'

'Of course I remembered,' she replied softly. It was those small intimate things that were impossible to forget.

They wended their way through Reception, which

was busy now with early evening visitors who had braved the elements to visit their loved ones.

Nan paused at the desk to ask Marge if there was any news of Hugh Latimer, but there wasn't. 'He's still in Theatre,' said Marge. 'According to one of the nurses to whom I spoke, pinning his leg together is like doing a jigsaw puzzle.' She looked at Callum, who was leaning on the desk. 'Dr Mac looks all in. Not surprising since he only arrived from down under yesterday morning. He must have awful jet lag.'

'You didn't tell me,' Nan said a few minutes later when he was sitting in a comfortable chair with a whisky in his hand, 'that you only flew in yesterday from Australia.'

'Haven't had a chance. I told the others in the bus but you and I had more important things to talk about. I've kept going on adrenalin and the excitement of seeing you again, but I'm afraid that I'm pooped now.'

Nan went through to the tiny kitchen to make tea. 'What you need right now is bed,' she called.

'Is that an offer?' replied Callum, slurring in his speech.

Nan returned with a tin full of biscuits. 'Eat as many as you can—your blood sugar's at rock bottom. And no,' she added softly, 'it's not an offer. You'll be staying with Aunt Janet while you're acting as locum—all our short-stay doctors do. Tom Barnard will be here soon to take you there.'

Callum sat up with a jerk. 'But I can't, not with Aunt Janet. Not after…'

Nan pressed him back in the chair with one hand and pushed a biscuit into his mouth with the other.

'Aunt Janet doesn't know everything that happened,' she soothed. 'And there's no reason why she should.'

Twenty minutes, half a glass of whisky and two mugs of sweet tea later, Tom arrived.

'Let's get going, Doc,' he said gruffly, taking Callum's arm and hauling him out of the chair. 'I've got your things in the bus. It's bed for you, you must be bushed. I'll get him back in the morning safe and sound, Matron,' he said, as Nan stood in the porch to see them off. 'A good sleep is all he needs.'

A good sleep is all I need, Nan thought a few hours later, wearily taking herself up to bed. She'd handed over to the night staff, and had phoned the hospital in Truro to learn that Hugh had come round after his op and was in Recovery. He was as well as could be expected.

Aunt Janet had phoned to say that Callum had been fed and watered and was in bed and fast asleep. She'd added, 'Tomorrow I want the truth and nothing but the truth from you, my girl, about you and this nice, sensible young man.'

'Yes, Aunty,' Nan had promised meekly. 'Talk to you tomorrow.'

CHAPTER FOUR

AS DAYS went, thought Nan, sinking at last into the soft comfort of her bed, it had been, to say the least, quite...extraordinary. No, extraordinary didn't really describe it. Starting with poor Hugh's fall and ending with Callum's arrival in a snowstorm—descending, as little Wendy would have it, like the Archangel Gabriel from heaven—it had been an explosive, stupendous, miraculous sort of day. But, then, it was Christmas—there couldn't have been a better time for miracles.

Now, for the first time in the long day, all was quiet. The patients for the moment were sleeping peacefully, which was what she meant to do as soon as her head touched the pillow.

The world outside was blanketed in snow. The wind had dropped and the special kind of silence that went with snow wrapped itself round the hospital.

The hot scented bath, which should have soothed, had instead triggered her into wakefulness, and a crystal-clear picture of the day she and Callum had first met sprang into her mind.

It had been ten years ago almost to the day...

Nan had heard Callum's voice before she'd seen him. She'd been in the middle of doing an internal on an expectant mum.

The voice had been deep and soft and gravelly with a faintly Scottish burr.

'Sean Connery eat your heart out.' That had been the word around the unit.

'Hi, love, how's it going?' Footsteps had crossed the room.

Love, indeed! She'd never met the man. The casually soft endearment and warmth in his voice hadn't matched up with what she'd been told about him.

For there had been no prize for guessing who it had been. The accent could only have belonged to Callum Mackintosh, the newly appointed anaesthetist registrar to Mr Fish's obs and gynae firm. Pretty good going at thirty. Rumour had had it that a consultant's post would be his within a year or so.

Rumour also had it that he was single-minded and ruthless where his career was concerned. He had, apparently, little time for the social whirl and none at all for more regular relationships. Well, that was according to the handful of intrepid and disappointed females who'd already tried to break through his armour.

Well, good for him, Nan had thought when she'd been put in the picture. Medicine's tough enough, without cluttering it up with untidy relationships. She felt that way herself about her own career. Nothing was going to stop her from getting to the top.

She was surprised, though, that he was here uninvited. She would have expected him to observe the rules, even the unwritten one that the delivery unit was midwife territory unless a doctor was called for. Even Mr Fish respected that. He valued his midwives and their special skills and instilled it into his medical team to do likewise.

So what was his newest recruit doing in *her* delivery room, unasked?

Oh, well, she'd forgive him this time. He probably meant no harm. She withdrew her gloved hand.

'A bit slow but we're getting there steadily.' She lifted her head and gave him a hard stare across the tented sheet draped over Lucy's knees.

The hard stare was wasted. He wasn't paying any attention to her but to a panting, grimacing Lucy gearing herself up for her next contraction. He had his hand on Lucy's shoulder. Nan saw his fingers tighten as the contraction built up. Everyone said that he was good with the patients, but this was above and beyond... These reassuring touches were the nurses' province. Quite apart from the unwritten rule, many doctors were only too ready to keep a low profile when women were in labour, unless asked to intervene. Not that he was exactly intervening.

He turned and she received the full force of a wide smile and twinkling hazel eyes. For some reason, they didn't go with the image that she'd had of him. 'Hope I'm not in the way,' he said. 'I'm Callum Mackintosh. I was in the department early this morning, having just done an epidural, when Lucy was admitted in the wee small hours. We had a little chat, didn't we, Luce?'

Luce! The diminutive of her name sounded oddly intimate and unlikely coming from him. Well, that might account for his tenderness toward the girl. The wee small hours, as he'd put it, did all sorts of things to the emotions, churned them up no end, turned strong men to jelly. And Dr Mackintosh looked to be one strong man, clearly at home in a kilt, tossing a caber or something else big and hefty. His shoulders could certainly take it—and the biceps visible beneath the cotton of his shirtsleeves. He was a walking advertisement for porridge or haggis.

Like a lot of big men, he would have been a sucker for someone like Lucy, alone and vulnerable and in distress. According to the report, she had come in unaccompanied. She looked vulnerable enough now. Heaven knew what she had looked like at three in the morning. If he was as good a doctor as rumour had it, no wonder he felt protective toward her.

Nan smiled back at him. He didn't look as if he'd been on night duty. His striped shirt, with the sleeves rolled up, was crisp and fresh, as was the white coat slung over his arm. He was all geared to start the day. His hair, damp and dark at the ends, was a glossy pale corn blond. He'd had a shower and smelt wonderful.

'You're not in the way,' she said.

She turned her attention back to Lucy. 'You're doing well, love. Do you want to walk around, sit out in the chair? You can take the gas and air with you.'

'I'll give you an arm,' offered Callum, his voice a throaty rumble.

Lucy turned her head restlessly from side to side on the pillows. 'I'll stay put,' she mumbled. 'My back's doing me in. I wish my mum would come.' Her lower lip trembled and big round tears rolled down her effort-reddened cheeks.

Nan tried to imagine what it was like to be sixteen and about to give birth, with no one of your own around for support. She'd seen it before, but somehow Lucy pulled at her heartstrings. Poor kid, it was bad enough that she was going to have to give up the baby, without going through this on her own. No wonder there wasn't much incentive to cope with the pains of labour. She said gently, 'When I rang her, she promised she'd come as soon as the babysitter arrived.'

'Oh, yeah,' groaned Lucy, rolling on her side and then back again, her face contorted with pain as another contraction built up.

'P'raps he won't let her come, just as he won't let me keep the baby, the b—' The last word came out on a strangled low-keyed shriek as the contraction gained momentum.

Callum caught Nan's eye as he stroked the girl's wispy hair back from her sweaty forehead. 'Epidural?' he mouthed, his hazel eyes dark with compassion.

I hope he never loses it, thought Nan. Would it die a death as he climbed to the top of the career ladder?

She nodded and waited for the contraction to subside, before speaking. 'Lucy, you know we talked about an epidural that would dull the pain by numbing you from the chest downwards. There's still time for you to have it. Dr Mackintosh is an anaesthetist—he could give it to you while he's here. It'll help, love, and won't hurt the baby if it's given now.'

Lucy stared at Nan as if she were mad. 'I told you, I can't stand needles,' she panted pettishly.

Callum bent low over the bed and smiled down at the frightened girl. He might have been a big brother. 'Make you a promise, Luce—you won't feel a thing. I'm a wizard at doing this.'

And big-headed with it, thought Nan. Spinals could be tricky, needing the patient's co-operation to keep absolutely still. To guarantee that it would be pain-free was a bit reckless, though it did vary from mum to mum and doctor to doctor. He didn't look reckless.

He had a calm face—a broad forehead, a wide mouth and straight eyebrows over those expressive hazel eyes. She looked at the strong, blunt fingers resting on the girl's shoulder, and suddenly felt hopeful. After all, it was nearly Christmas—perhaps a small miracle was due.

She touched Lucy's other shoulder. 'He is good, you know. Like he said, he's a wizard.'

Lucy's face screwed up. Another contraction was on the way. 'OK,' she gasped when it was over, 'I'll have this epi thing, but it'd better not hurt.'

Nan moved the trolley with the epidural equipment near the bed. Callum put on his white coat, scrubbed his hands and pulled on the sterile gloves she had ready for him.

'I'm going to put up a drip first, Lucy, and run liquid through a tube in your arm to prevent you becoming dehydrated.' He produced another of his reassuring smiles. 'And I'm a wizard at doing this, too. You'll feel the tiniest scratch.'

Lucy screwed her eyes shut. 'Go on, then, get on with it,' she muttered.

While Nan set a stand in position and hung a bag of glucose and saline on the hook Callum, with practised fingers, found a suitable vein, slid in the needle and attached the plastic tubing to the bag. Slowly he opened up the connection between the two tubes, allowing the fluid to drip through gradually, adjusting it until it reached the rate he wanted.

Lucy gasped. 'There's another one coming.' Her face contorted as a contraction gripped her.

Nan timed it by her fob watch. 'Nice, steady breaths,' she murmured. 'That's it. Well done.'

Callum raised his eyebrows. 'Now, I think,' he said, as Lucy's muscles began to relax.

Nan nodded. 'We're ready to start the epidural, Lucy,' she said. 'Roll towards me and pull your knees up as far as you can. Make yourself into a ball.' She slid her arms round the girl's back to help her turn. 'Now you must hold still whilst the tube is being inserted into your spine. You'll have to grit your teeth if you have a contraction. It won't take too long and will be well worth it in the end.'

Lucy lay curled up as still as a statue as Callum swabbed her back with an antiseptic agent from the waist downward. He then administered a local anaesthetic around her spine in the lumbar and lower dorsal area. It took a few minutes for the local to work. Then his rounded but sensitive fingertips felt for the right spot between the vertebrae and smoothly slid in the hollow needle. Once it was in place, he threaded the fine catheter through the needle.

Nan thought, He *is* a wizard. It was the smoothest spinal she'd ever seen. He secured the tubing in place with a gauze pad, then very slowly injected a measured dose of nerve-numbing anaesthetic through the fine plastic tubing.

'All done, love,' he said when he'd emptied the syringe. 'I'm leaving the tubing in place so that we can top up the anaesthetic if necessary.'

Lucy was breathing rapidly and beginning to get restless as another contraction began to build, and all the gritting of teeth in the world couldn't stop her moving. Nan rolled her gently onto her back, checking that the fluid was still running freely. 'The painkiller won't begin to work straight away, Lucy, but it will cut in quite soon. Now, try to go with this contraction, don't fight it.'

Perhaps the idea of getting pain relief helped, but when the contraction ended Lucy panted, 'That was a bit better.' She managed a weak smile. 'Thanks, Doctor, you're good, you are.'

Callum returned her smile, his eyes crinkling at the corners. 'You're welcome,' he said, moving to the door. He transferred his smile to Nan. Even across the room she felt warmed by it and her heart thumped unevenly.

Ridiculous, she told herself, things like this don't happen in real life, only in the pages of books. No way was she going to join the band of thwarted females he'd apparently offended. A hospital Romeo she could do without. She wasn't lusting after him or anybody.

He was saying something...

'I'll get out of your way now, Staff Nurse, but you only have to bleep if you need me, though I'll be in Theatre for part of the day. If I'm not available, and Lucy's anaesthetic needs to be topped up, Jeff will be around.'

As quietly as he seemed to do everything, he opened the door, slid his large person quietly out of the room and was gone.

'He's nice, isn't he?' murmured Lucy. 'Pity he had to go.'

'Very nice,' confirmed Nan, as she tidied up the trolley, disposing of used bits and pieces in a plastic bag whilst silently agreeing that it was a pity he'd had to go.

Cursing herself for having such an unprofessional thought, she dismissed it from her mind and sat down to fill in her charts. She listed the medication that had been administered and the time it had been given. She noted temperature, pulse and respirations, degree of pain, duration of contractions and the time between each. There were duplicates of everything these days—the paperwork was horrendous.

The room was suddenly very quiet. Lucy was almost dozing, which did sometimes happen after an epidural.

There was a tap at the door. Nan opened it and a tall, thin woman, so obviously an older version of Lucy that it could only be her mother, entered timidly.

'I'm Mrs Brooks,' she whispered, 'Lucy's mum. I'm sorry I couldn't get here earlier. Is she all right?' She herself looked absolutely whacked and close to tears.

Nan steered her to a chair by the bed. 'She's fine, just dozing because she's had an epidural to help control the pain. Take her hand. She'll be so pleased to see you.' She added. 'Can I get you something to drink? Tea, coffee?'

'Thank you. Coffee would be nice, with milk and sugar, please.'

Nan whisked out of the room and along the corridor to the office, where a coffee percolator bubbled aromatically away, a much-blessed gift from an ex-patient who'd recognised that the midwives worked erratic hours and often couldn't take normal breaks.

She gulped down half a mug of black coffee and sugar, before returning to the delivery room with a mug for Mrs Brooks.

Mrs Brooks had her arms round Lucy and was rocking her backwards and forwards. Lucy was laughing and crying at the same time. 'Oh, Nurse, isn't it great? Mum's going to help me keep the baby,' she burst out when Lucy entered the room. 'She's sent *him* packing.'

Though applauding Mrs Brooks's action, Nan privately wondered how they were going to manage. And who was he? Husband, partner, boyfriend? Nan flashed mother and daughter a smile. In the few minutes she'd been away, it was amazing how the atmosphere in the room had changed.

Lucy was still a frightened young woman, giving birth to her first baby, but despair had turned to hope. Pain had some meaning, there was now a goal to aim for. It was in the young girl's eyes—they positively glowed. For just an instant Nan almost envied her. In a few hours she would have a baby of her own to love and cherish.

With a mental shrug, reminding herself that she was a career-woman on her way to the top of her profession, and having a baby wasn't an option, Nan said, 'Oh, Lucy, I'm so pleased for you, love.' She handed the coffee to Mrs Brooks. 'Now, I'm just going to check you again and listen to your baby's heartbeat. You're about due for another contraction, but it might not feel as strong as before on account of the epidural so you must push if I tell you to.'

Everything was as it should have been. The baby's heartbeat was strong, the head perfectly positioned for a normal presentation. Lucy was an ideal patient, doing everything asked of her. The euphoria brought on by her mother's presence, and the knowledge that she could keep her baby, continued to buoy her up, although by mid-afternoon she was beginning to get very tired.

Madge Thorn, the obstetric registrar, called in at

three-thirty to see how things were progressing. She announced herself satisfied. 'But give a shout,' she told Nan, 'if things haven't really moved in the next half-hour. I don't want that baby hanging about much longer.'

Ten minutes later there was a tap at the door, and Callum slid into the room, though he remained by the door. He was wearing blue cotton theatre pyjamas, the round cap perched on his head, a mask dangling from his neck.

'May I come in, Staff?' he asked, his tone meek enough to make Nan smile.

Nan took a deep breath and nodded. 'You may,' she said, 'if Lucy doesn't mind.'

Lucy gave a tired smile. 'Of course not. Mum, this is the nice doctor who gave me my epi—epidural.'

Callum crossed to the bed and shook hands with Mrs Brooks. 'I'm so glad you could get here,' he said. 'She's a brave girl, your daughter.'

'She is that,' replied Mrs Brooks.

Nan had her hands flat on Lucy's abdomen. She pressed gently. 'There'a another contraction coming, Lucy. This is a big one. Push and go on pushing. Don't give up, love... Go on, push, your baby's nearly here.' Lucy pushed and pushed.

'It's coming, the baby's coming,' called out Mrs Brooks.

Nan repositioned her hands, ready to steer the small creature out into the world—and all of a sudden it was there. The head emerged, quickly followed by tiny shoulders and the rest of the body. A squirming, slippery bundle, with black hair slicked down with blood and mucus and a red, puckered-up angry face.

There was a moment's silence, and then a mewing sound, and then a lusty wail.

'It's a little girl,' murmured Mrs Brooks happily. 'Oh, Luce, we've got a little girl. She's beautiful.'

Callum met Nan's eyes and they smiled at each other. And Nan knew that he was thinking as she was. The baby wasn't beautiful—new baby's weren't—but they were special, awe-inspiring, enough to send a shiver down one's spine, having made the most important journey of their lives. Nan handed the little girl to her mother who, young as she was, knew instinctively what to do. She cuddled it and crooned to it, forging the bond that would last a lifetime.

Nan said impulsively, 'I'm glad you were here.'

'I wouldn't have missed it for anything,' said Callum. 'A happy outcome to a rotten start. I've seen plenty of Caesareans but few natural births except in my training days. Usually once I've set up the epidural I'm superfluous. I'll have to be off now, but I'll come back later to remove the spinal set. I think the drip should remain *in situ* for a few more hours.'

Nan nodded. She was concentrating on easing the passage of the placenta, pressing one flat palm on Lucy's abdomen. 'Another push, Lucy,' she encouraged. 'The last one.'

Her eyes still on her baby, Lucy pushed and the placenta slid into the dish Nan had to hand.

Callum moved to the door. 'Will you still be on duty, Staff, when I come back?'

So formal, and yet... 'Till seven,' said Nan. 'And the name's Nannette Winters, Nan for short.'

His smile lit up his face, lit up the room. 'I'll remember that,' he said in his soft, throaty voice.

It was the beginning, as she had known it would

be from the moment she'd stared at him over Lucy's tented knees, of a very special relationship. It grew and flourished as Christmas and New Year came and went. Pristine white snow, which had carpeted the city streets round the hospital, turned to grey slush and then to rain-washed, glistening pavements.

Spring took over and the heath near the hospital came to life, sprouting tender green leaves and bright new grass. They moved in together into a tiny studio flat that overlooked the trees and acres of green and the rooftops of north London. It cost the earth, but as Callum commented drily as they stood at the window that first evening, 'Considering it's next door to heaven, it's a bargain.'

Then he wrapped his arms round her and kissed her upturned face. Still showering her with kisses, he edged her to the wide divan bed.

Nan smiled into the darkness, remembering how they had made love on their newly acquired bed. 'It's ready to be christened,' Callum had murmured between kisses, lowering them both down onto the springy mattress.

She sucked in a deep breath. In those days all their kissing had ended up with them on the bed, making love. And what kisses they had been. In books, kisses were described as firm or butterfly or brushed. None of those words had applied to Callum's kisses. They had been just that—Callum kisses—unique and precious, never to be imitated.

It had been unthinkable then that their love should ever have ended, but it had by high summer and the heath had turned brown as if in sympathy.

A heavy sigh shuddered through Nan and she turned off the mental picture. She didn't want to remember those last few days when love, or whatever it was, had turned sour and they'd both said hurtful things to each other. Could those words ever be unsaid?

Purposefully, she plumped up her pillows and lay down at attention, flat on her back, crossing her hands over her bosom. No point in dwelling on the past and what might have been. The present was what mattered. This Christmas, when fate had miraculously brought them together again in an isolated Cornish coastal village, cut off from the big wide world. This was the reality, the here and now.

She had a hospital to run and a new—old—doctor to help her run it. And Aunt Janet to answer to.

CHAPTER FIVE

CALLUM wouldn't let Nan sleep. Her bed was warm and comfortable, she was dog tired, but every time she began to drop off her mind went into overdrive, going like the clappers over yesterday's events—from poor old Hugh's fall to Callum's arrival in the helicopter.

Dear Hugh, lying in the rescuscitation ward, dopey with drugs after his hours in Theatre. They hadn't been able to tell her much when she'd last rung, just that putting his leg together had been tricky and that there'd been some bleeding into the surrounding tissues. They were worried about infection and he was being drip-fed massive amounts of antibiotics.

Nan sighed into the darkness. Poor, darling Hugh. God knew how long he was going to be out of action. Meanwhile, Tintore had Callum... At last she began to doze.

The video-like flashback recalling in detail her first meeting with Callum ten years before sprang into focus again, sending her heart and pulses racing and her stomach churning. She sat up in bed and pressed the palms of her hands against her eyes in an attempt to blot out the picture of the younger Callum, with his cheerful face and laughing eyes. It didn't work—it was indelibly printed on her mind.

Yet strangely the moment she was properly awake and fully alert, it wasn't the younger man but the mature forty-year-old Callum, with his blond hair bleached by the Australian sun, who sprang to mind. The Callum who had descended from the helicopter yesterday.

Nan got up early and was in her office before even Marge had arrived behind the reception desk.

The first thing she did was to phone Truro for the latest news of Hugh. She got the usual spiel from a tired night nurse. He'd had a comfortable night—not very likely after the extensive surgery he'd undergone, Nan thought, however much morphine they'd pumped into him—and if all was well he was to be transferred to Orthopaedics from Intensive Care later that morning.

'Tell him I rang,' said Nan, hoping that her message would get through. 'And tell him all is well at this end.'

She put the receiver down and gazed out of the window. It was still dark, but lit by the external lights she could see that there had been another fall of snow during the night, laying a smooth, sparkling icing over the car park and covering up yesterday's tyre tracks. The snow gave her a fillip of childish excitement, as it always did, and in spite of it being the cause of Hugh's fall and Callum's appearance to turn her ordered way of life upside down she was glad that it was going to be a white Christmas.

The postal van churned slowly up the drive to the front door. It was followed by the ambulance-bus driven by Tom. To her surprise, and sending a great wave of tingling pleasure, which she couldn't suppress, coursing through her, Callum was with him. After his long day yesterday, she hadn't really expected him in till later.

The postman disappeared beneath the portico to deliver a sackful of letters and parcels to reception. Night Sister would receive it if Marge hadn't arrived yet.

She frowned. How had the post got through? Was it local village stuff or mail delivered yesterday before The Lane had been closed off by snow? Unless the air ambulance, flying in Callum and taking Hugh to hospital, had dropped it off. That was strictly against the rules, of course, but sometimes rules were made to be broken.

Organising Hugh's removal from the bus, she'd been too busy to notice if anything else had arrived. But it was the sort of occasion when, in the interests of common sense, the rules were sometimes bent, and authority sensibly turned a blind eye to the fact that the ambulance was being used to fly in mail. Robin had done it before when the weather had isolated the village.

She watched as Callum climbed out of the bus with a bag full of gear, and her heart pitter-pattered like a moth in a lampshade. She stood rooted to the spot, conscious that she should move if she didn't want him to see her, but somehow she was unable to do so.

He looked along the terrace, saw her at the window and gave her an extravagant salute and an ironic half-bow...as if he'd known she'd be there, waiting to catch a glimpse of him. It was the sort of gesture typical of the old Callum and apparently was true of the *new* Callum, too—if there was such an animal...

A new Callum with all the good attributes of the old and none of the bad—was it possible? There had been glimpses yesterday of a maturer, kinder man with a softer side to him. He'd always been kind to the patients, a jolly doctor who'd cheered them up and had made them laugh, and no one had ever doubted his medical expertise. And women had fallen like ninepins to his charm, but beneath that polished veneer there had been a ruthless man, as she had discovered.

A man who had put his career first all the time, who had refused to budge an inch when she had needed him.

Did that ruthless man still exist? He'd said that he'd changed, but in what way? He'd been as good as ever yesterday with the patients, but that meant nothing. Nan sat down at her desk and struggled to get a grip on herself. 'Don't make a fool of yourself, Winters, not again,' she whispered.

There was a tap on the door. For a moment she held her breath—and then let it go in a rush. It hadn't been Callum's decisive knock.

'Come in.'

It was Night Sister Helen Bright, come to fill her in on the night's happenings. Nan waved her into a chair. 'You look whacked. Sit there, I'll make coffee. Instant, I'm afraid. Haven't got round to perking any yet.' She disappeared into the tiny kitchen, returning a couple of minutes later with two steaming mugs. 'Now, give me the low-down. I'll go through the full report with Joyce later.'

'Little Marie's had a lot of pain. She's had her maximum dosage of anti-inflammatory agents and analgesics. I think she needs something stronger—perhaps our new man will agree.' Helen took a sip of coffee and arched an eyebrow at Nan. 'He's quite something, isn't he? Tom introduced me. An old friend of yours, I believe. Did you know him very well?'

'How on earth do you know that we worked together in the past? He's only just walked in through the front door.'

Helen looked vague. 'Oh, someone I met in the stores yesterday afternoon. It's pretty common knowledge, Nan, you know what this place is like.'

'Full of Nosy Parkers—beats M.I.5. into a cocked hat,' said Nan laconically. 'But I'll ask him about Marie. If there's anything that will help her, Callum will know about it. On the spot with anything new that's available—he's good. Now, who else do we need to talk about?'

'The twins haven't had a brilliant night, coughing and wheezing. Too much excitement and dust, decorating the tree, I guess. They each had a session on the nebuliser and settled better afterwards, but they're a bit low this morning so I told them to stay in bed for their breakfast. The rest of the kids were fine.'

'Old Henry?'

'Sleeping like a babe at the moment, but had the shivers at two o'clock this morning so we warmed him up again slowly. His six-o'clock temp, pulse, respirations and blood pressure were all within normal limits. Young Henry rang at ten last night and will be in this morning. His language concerning his father's activities yesterday—out hunting stray sheep in the dark—had to be heard to be believed. He's going to give the old boy a right bollocking when he visits.'

Nan chuckled. 'They're a right pair, aren't they? Not much to choose between them when it comes to being tough. You'd think, to hear young Henry, that he was a strapping young lad, not seventy-something. Now, anything else on the agenda?'

'Nothing much. Poor old Alice Snelling had her usual bowel problems. I'm afraid the laundry aren't going to be too pleased—we had to change her bed three times. I wish some of these clever bods who keep coming up with miraculous cures for this and that could sort out incontinence. But there you go. The big pharmaceutical firms aren't much interested. There's nothing glamorous about incontinence, is there?'

'Nope!' Nan shook her head. 'Now, off you go, Helen. See you tonight. Thanks for looking after my family—now go and look after your own.'

Helen's eyes twinkled as she got up and moved to the door. 'I'm away. Have fun, renewing acquaintance with you know who, and bring me up to date on the state of play tonight.'

Nan pointed at the door. 'Out, begone, disappear,' she said with pretended ferociousness.

'I'm gone already,' Helen said with a laugh, opening the door.

Callum was standing outside, his hand raised to knock.

'Visitor for you, Matron,' said Helen demurely. Fluttering her eyes at Callum as she slid past him, she added, 'We meet again, Doctor.'

Nan was astonished to see her somewhat staid night sister actually flirting. It was just as she'd feared yesterday. As inevitably as day followed night, Callum was going to charm all her female staff into willing slaves. It could be amusing, but in a small community like Tintore it could be dangerous, get out of hand, and someone might get hurt.

She had better warn him again to go easy with spreading that charm of his around—remind him that this wasn't London but a Cornish village where everyone knew everyone.

Callum turned his head and watched Helen walk away from him then turned back to Nan. He grinned. 'Are all your staff born actors?' he asked.

'Only in response to someone like you,' she replied, trying to keep the breathiness out of her voice. She waved him into her office. 'Come in, Callum. How did you sleep?'

'Like the proverbial top after Aunt Janet had fed me and given me a grilling.'

He sat down opposite her, his grin widening, his eyes glowing, speaking volumes that he didn't try to hide. 'She's a great old girl, a little less acerbic than I remember her at my one and only brief meeting with her when she came up to Town.' He spoke quite naturally as if that meeting had been weeks ago rather than ten years ago. 'But then she'd been giving me the once-over as a prospective partner for her beloved niece.'

Nan looked at his smiling face. He was so calm, so at ease. Janet couldn't have probed too deeply or he wouldn't have been able to look like that—surely he would have been absolutely shattered. 'She doesn't know the whole story, Callum, only that we had a...a disagreement and decided to part. I didn't want to hurt her by telling her—'

'What an utter heel I was.' The smile left his face. 'No, I realised that. If you had, she wouldn't have let me cross her threshold.'

Callum got up and strode about the room. He stopped with his hands planted on her desk and leaned forward, his breath fanning her cheeks, his eyes devouring her, pleading with her. 'And I'm grateful to you for that, love. That might have been too big a bridge to mend and now that I'm here that's what I want to do.

'Nan.' His soft voice with the Scottish burr almost choked on her name. 'Nan, I didn't understand, didn't appreciate how ill she was or how much she meant to you. All I wanted was to get on with my career. Nothing else seemed to matter. And I thought that you felt the same. If I hadn't been head-hunted for that particular job in the US...'

'Another job would have come up, Callum.' Her voice was dry and matter-of-fact. 'Let's face it, we were both hell bent on climbing the career ladder and, who knows, if positions had been reversed I might have walked out on you. How would you have felt if either of your parents had been at death's door and I wouldn't put my career on hold for a short while so that you could be with them?'

He cupped her chin, his eyes only inches from hers. 'I would have felt utterly betrayed by you,' he said thickly. 'Nan, I have no excuses to offer. I honestly couldn't see *then* why you should sacrifice yourself to look after Aunt Janet, and I certainly couldn't see why you expected me to wait around. I was selfish and cruel and at thirty should have known better. To my regret I didn't, but I do now, my love.'

He murmured the words 'my love' like a caress. His mouth was close—the mouth that had once showered her with kisses. She wanted to trace the outline of it with her finger...until she remembered where she was and jerked back in her chair. She had come perilously near to touching his lips, here in the middle of her office at the beginning of a working day.

Dear God, what was he going to make her do next? It was as if he were manipulating her like a puppet on a string. Yet he wouldn't do that, would he? He sounded so sincere, and he had always been that. He'd never made promises that he hadn't been able to keep. In fact, he'd been totally blunt and honest. That had been the hardness beneath the fun-loving surface, the hardness that he'd just referred to as cruelty.

It took her a moment or two to recover. She was breathing in and out rapidly. He was still leaning on her desk, his well-kept blunt fingers, which were magical when they examined a patient or gave an injection or twiddled the dozens of knobs on his lifesaving machine, were splayed out on the polished surface.

She remembered that it wasn't only that fascinating accent of his which had drawn her like a magnet, but his strong, clever hands.

She suddenly found herself giggling out loud, really giggling, like a young girl rather than a very mature woman. 'And a matron to boot,' she choked out through her giggles.

Callum pushed himself up from the desk and stared at her as if she'd gone mad. 'Nan, what the devil's the matter with you?'

By now, tears were rolling down Nan's cheeks. Part of her was aware that it was a kind of relief mechanism after all that had happened in the last twenty-four hours, but part of it was because the thought that had just struck her seemed to her just plain funny.

'You're hysterical,' said Callum, moving round the

desk, swivelling her chair round and gripping her shoulders.

Nan looked up at him with glittering eyes and shook her head slightly. She pulled a tissue from the box, wiped her eyes and blew her nose.

'A little perhaps,' she agreed with a smile. 'It was a thought that I had that struck me as funny.'

Callum kept hold of her shoulders. He didn't look convinced, just concerned. 'Share it with me.'

She steadied her voice, though there was still laughter there. 'Well, men are supposed to be leg men or breast men or get turned on by some part of a woman's anatomy, and some women go for buttocks or shoulders or thighs, while I, nice, prim Matron Winters—I go for voices and hands.' She twinkled up at him—she still thought it was funny.

All at once, a great tidal wave of optimism washed over her. She didn't know whether it was because it was Christmas and the tree sparkling in the hall, or the snow, or Callum's presence—perhaps it was a little of each—but she was suddenly sure that everything was going to turn out 'hunky-dorey', as Aunt Janet would have said.

His hands relaxed on her shoulders and he brought them up to stroke a few curly strands of hair from her face. He was smiling broadly.

'I can see how that would have amused you,' he said softly, affectionately, 'with your zany sense of humour.' He tilted his head down and kissed her. 'But I don't go with prim. Isn't there any other part of me that you fancy beside my voice and hands?' His eyebrows were peaked triangles, his mouth wore a lopsided grin.

She ignored the provocative innuendo. 'Your feet,'

she murmured. 'I always thought that you had nice feet, large but well shaped.'

He uttered a brief laugh and then looked serious. 'Nan, we do need to talk. I'm sorry that I was bushed last night and couldn't talk, as we'd planned, but talk we must. We need to fill in ten years. It's obvious that we've both changed.' He smoothed her tawny gold hair and the braided chignon just visible beneath the scrap of lace that was her cap. 'Your hair used to be short, for one thing, beautifully cut and business-like. What made you grow it?'

'A need to look older than twenty-five and impress the natives so that I could take over as Matron. Joyce managed for a few months whilst Aunt Janet was having her treatment, but when it became clear that Janet would never be fit enough to return to full-time control she wanted to opt out.'

'"I'm a good second in command," she informed me, "but I don't want to step into Janet's shoes. You're the person to do that." We've worked harmoniously together ever since. It's been a brilliant partnership, but…'

Callum dragged a chair to Nan's side. 'But?'

All her senses stirred. It was lovely to feel him so close, his thigh almost touching hers, warm and sturdy and familiar. He used to have a ticklish spot just behind his knee—did he still have it? Just in time she stopped her hand from straying…

'But?' he repeated.

'But it wasn't an easy decision to make,' she murmured softly. 'It was much bigger than the decision to look after Aunty, which was a blood-thicker-than-water thing and quite straightforward. There was no contest. A combination of loving her since I'd been a small child and the fact that she was my only living relative, it left me with no option and no desire to opt out. But this was different. I owed nothing to the village or the hospital. I made up my mind to say, no, I would stay till Aunt Janet recovered, then I'd be off.'

She clenched her hands, her knuckles white. Callum covered them. 'So what happened to make you change your mind?'

Nan frowned, looking back, trying to be honest. 'A number of things. Helping out briefly whilst the trustees were trying to appoint someone else. They interviewed any number of unsuitable candidates. We had a virulent flu epidemic which finished off a lot of the oldies—you can see their graves down in the churchyard. A whole lot of them died that year. There was no way I could leave them whilst that was going on...' Her voice trailed off.

'But there was one specific thing that swung the balance, wasn't there?' Callum guessed, kissing her white knuckles.

'Fighting one night for a small child's life—Polly's, actually...'

'Pretty little Polly Bowen who takes care of the kids and who took the mickey out of me when I arrived?'

'*That* pretty little Polly.' Nan smiled. 'She was eight and developed measles, the life-and-death sort of measles that we rarely see now, thank God. The Lane was washed away and the weather was so bad that the air ambulance couldn't get through for three days. Hugh Latimer and I, occasionally helped by Aunt Janet, who was just getting back on her feet, together with Joyce and the other trained staff barrier-nursed her for about seventy-two hours night and day.'

'The night watches,' said Callum. 'They're the ones that do things to you.'

'Yes. Anyway, as you can see, Polly survived. Her brush with hospital life decided her on a nursing career, particularly with children. The hospital trust paid for her to do a two-year nursery nurse's course, at which she shone. We decided to engage her to work specifically with the children, though supervised by a staff nurse to cover medical or surgical problems when necessary. As you see, the arrangement has worked well.'

'Brilliantly. She obviously has a flair for her work. And that emergency made you decide to stay?'

'Yes, although I thought in terms of a couple of years—' her eyes met his '—while I was getting over you, Callum.' She was trembling. It was her first admission of how desperately she had been hurt by him, and how long the hurt had lasted.

His eyes were full of contrition. He rubbed his thumbs across her inner wrists as he used to do. 'Nan, let me—'

There was a sharp rap on the door and Marge came in before Nan could invite her or Callum could release her hands. Usually totally unruffled, Marge was looking worried.

'Just had a call from Mrs Horton. Doc Horton's gone down with what sounds like a really bad dose of flu. Mrs H. doesn't panic. I promised someone would call pronto. I said he didn't look well yesterday, Nan. If he needs nursing, I don't see how Mrs H. can manage.'

Both Nan and Callum stood up. 'Have you got your medical bag with you, Callum?' Nan asked briskly.

'I have. It's in the day unit, ready for me to do a surgery.'

'Then fetch it. You're going on your first home visit and I'm going with you. Marge, track down Tom and the bus—we'll go in that—and be ready if Doc Horton needs to be brought back here.'

Nan introduced Callum to Dr and Mrs Horton when they arrived at Tallboys some twenty minutes later. The old doctor could hardly speak.

'I'm afraid that your chest is pretty solid, sir,' said Callum, after he had examined him. 'You've flu—or something akin to it—and pneumonia. I need to pump you full of antibiotics and fluids and oxygen for a few days, and take some X-rays and arrange for you to have physio. I guess that's what you would do faced with the same symptoms.'

Nan could have hugged him for bringing the older doctor into the discussion and not treating him as a lay patient.

The handsome, grey-haired doctor produced a grim sort of smile and said hoarsely, 'What you're saying is that you want me hospitalised.'

'How did you guess?' asked Callum wryly.

'One gets to know the lingo after fifty years,' Dr Horton muttered, and began to doze.

'He's a great old chap,' Callum said an hour later as he and Nan walked down the corridor.

They had seen the doctor safely installed in a comfortable room, separated by the small staffroom from the other rooms in the long-stay unit. He was connected to a drip to pump in much-needed fluid to prevent him becoming dehydrated, and he'd been given a double starter dose of an umbrella of antibiotics. Mrs Horton, looking pale but determined, was sitting beside him, holding his hand and being fussed over by Eve, the nurse who was to special the doctor.

'Yes. He and Aunt Janet set up the hospital about forty years ago, converting the manor house and incorporating the almshouses. They got it off the ground, set the foundations for what it is today.' Nan laid a hand on Callum's arm, her eyes fearful. 'How's he doing, Callum? He's pretty sick, isn't he? Is he going to make it?'

He squeezed her hand where it lay on his arm. 'Yup—he is pretty sick. We're going to have to pull out all the stops on this one, Nan. Hope that it's a bacterial bug rather than a virus, and will respond to the antibiotics.'

'And pray that it doesn't spread,' muttered Nan grimly, remembering the epidemic of ten years ago.

'Amen to that,' said Callum. He glanced at his watch. 'Bit late for my surgery. I'll have some explaining to do.'

'Don't bother.' Nan managed a laugh. 'Myrtle Keen, your nurse-cum-receptionist, will have made your excuses and everyone will know that Doc H. is ill and you've been examining him. Just expect to be bombarded with questions as to how he's doing and what treatment you're giving him. You're in for the third degree.'

Callum chuckled. 'Patient confidentiality?' he queried.

Nan's mood lightened, feeling suddenly that if anyone could pull the old doctor through Callum could.

As an anaesthetist he was a wizard at mixing gases so why not at mixing antibiotics and painkillers and whatever else was necessary?

She laughed easily this time. 'Doc Horton won't mind. Patient confidentiality hardly exists in Tintore, but when it's necessary Hugh and I take avoiding action and make it up as we go along. You'll soon catch on. Good luck with your first surgery. I'm off to do my rounds. By the way, if you have to do any visits, Tom will take you in the bus.'

They stood for a moment side by side near the bottom of the stairs, gazing around what had once been the great hall of the manor house and was now the impressive reception room. There were pictures on the walls, originals, mostly bold flower pictures or misty seascapes.

'Painted by local artists,' guessed Callum.

Nan nodded. 'Like most Cornish villages, we have our artists' colony.'

Though the hall was large, it was inviting and homely, with its pictures and wall-to-wall carpeting. Marge and the assistant receptionist, Kate, sat behind the polished desk that faced the massive front door, a sort of welcoming committee. They were both on the phone, but waved and smiled at Nan and Callum.

Nurses and care assistants bustled about, carrying trays, giving an arm to a tottery patient, pushing wheelchairs. Several of them smiled and nodded in their direction and then went about their business.

'You know,' murmured Callum, 'this must be one of the few places left where people actually smile and seem to be pleased to see one another. I noticed it directly I landed yesterday. Everyone was so willing.'

He placed a hand on Nan's shoulder. It felt warm and heavy through her uniform dress.

I should step away, she thought, but I don't want to. He read her thoughts, as he had always done. 'They won't think it strange,' he whispered, his breath stirring the ringlets of tawny hair that had strayed from the confines of her lacy cap. 'They know we're old friends.' His hand continued to rest on her shoulder as if it had a right to be there.

Callum was right. No one was taking much notice of them, everyone was going about his or her business. They might be curious, but they were also polite. No one stared, no one presumed to invade their space.

Reception was always busy at this time of morning, with visitors arriving and cleaners polishing. Today Dave the orderly was busy framing the doors and windows with bunches of holly and ivy.

'He does it every year,' said Nan, giving Dave a wave. 'Comes in specially the day before Christmas Eve to finish the decorating of the public rooms. Later today he'll set up the nativity figures beside the tree, large wooden models carved by his grandfather and dressed by the friends of the hospital, and by tomorrow night everything will be perfect for the carol service.'

Aromatic scents wafted through the air from the direction of the corridor leading to the kitchens.

Callum sniffed appreciatively. 'Something smells good.'

'The last cook-up before D-Day...'

'Don't tell me.' He wrinkled his nose. 'I detect mince pies, sausage rolls, apple turnovers, sausages and bacon and onion pasties.' He breathed in again deeply, 'Ah, and cheesy things...'

Nan couldn't take her eyes from his face. It was bright and alight and teasing and... 'You've forgotten mushrooms and other veggie things,' she breathed. She felt faint and elated and raring to go, all at the same time.

He grinned, his wide lovely grin. 'Sherlock would be ashamed of me,' he said.

Later she would wonder what had prompted her, but at the time it seemed to be the most natural thing in the world to do. She stretched up and kissed him sweetly on the mouth. 'You'd better get on with your surgery,' she said softly. 'We'll have lunch in my flat when you're finished.'

CHAPTER SIX

'THAT,' said Callum, laying aside his soup spoon, 'was delicious, Can't beat home-made onion soup and warm rolls on a day like this. There was always a potful on the go when I was a wee kid. I could smell it long before I got into the house, cold and hungry after trudging home from school in the snow. Mum would be there in the kitchen, ready to ladle it out.' He smiled slightly.

Did he mean to sound so nostalgic and wistful and, in spite of the smile, sad almost? His lean, tanned face looked wistful, too, and some of the dance had gone out of his hazel eyes. He thrust his fingers through his bleached hair, ruffling it up. It was unfashionably long and curling against the roll neck of his black sweater. The white on black made him look very handsome and rather distinguished.

Nan found herself itching to tangle her fingers in the thick, nearly white hair resting on his collar—and she wanted to kiss him again, as she had when they'd been standing at the foot of the stairs. Only this time it would be a long, comforting, lingering kiss...

Stop it! she commanded herself. Any minute now you're going to make an almighty fool of yourself, just as you did all those years ago. This wistfulness, this vulnerability, is simply another facet of his charm and charisma.

She stood up abruptly and picked up their empty soup plates. 'I'll fetch the pudding.'

He nodded vaguely, as if he had a lot on his mind. But what? she wondered as she put the plates in the sink. Had his nostalgic reference to the onion soup triggered off memories—unhappy memories?

When he'd returned from his house calls a short time ago, with an apology for being late, he'd seemed his usual cheerful self. 'Well, nobody died on me,' he'd said with a wry smile when Nan had asked how his morning had gone. 'Though I have my doubts about being able to save one patient a few toes, even perhaps part of a foot. Some of the toes are ulcerated to the bone, and rather whiffy to say the least. She's a bright, middle-aged lady who has—'

'Raynaud's syndrome,' Nan had interrupted. 'And her circulation has nearly come to a stop, as it does every winter. Glenda Woods. Hugh was trying to persuade her to come in for a few days so that we could give her high-pressure care and increase her vascular dilators under supervision. He didn't pull any punches—told her that if she didn't, she'd end up in Truro General, having her toes off. But she won't leave the stock and domestic animals till her husband gets back, and with this weather...' She'd shrugged.

They were standing only inches apart in her small hall, and Callum raised his eyebrows and laughed down at her—one of his soft throaty laughs, which made his eyes dance and crinkle up at the corners, a laugh which at that moment seemed just for her. His hair had been tinted by the light from the orange-shaded wall lamp that lit the hall, turning it into a glowing halo. Like a knight in a children's story book, she thought, tingling from head to toe and wishing that he would kiss her.

It was a warm, intimate, loving moment, though they were talking cold, clinical shop.

'I keep forgetting,' he said, 'that everyone knows everyone in Tintore and is well informed about everyone else's health. You were bound to know. Even Tom told me that Glenda's condition was in the family. Apparently, her mother had an above-knee amputation.'

'That was five years ago. She died a couple of years afterwards of an embolism. Like Glenda, she was a stubborn old thing, but happy. By the way, did you get my message about little Marie?'

Callum struggled out of his lambswool-lined car coat and hung it on the old-fashioned hatstand, then spun round and cupped her chin with firm hands. He kissed the tip of her nose.

'I did. I went to see her before I went out on my visits. I've upped her painkillers and I'm giving some thought about gentle massage with pain-relieving oils. Have you got a massage or aromatherapist in the village?'

'No, afraid not. Even if we could find one, I'm not sure that the hospital could cover that as we've got a physiotherapist.'

'But physio and aromatherapy or massage are three different disciplines.'

Nan smiled. 'You and I know that, but I have a feeling that the board will see one as a necessity, the other as...'

He smiled, too. 'A rather risqué, over-the-top extra. Perhaps if I chatted to Aunt Janet and some of the others, convince them that I've seen it applied effectively to similar cases to little Marie's. Pity old Doc

Horton is laid low. I've a feeling he might have been on our side.'

'Mrs Horton may be,' said Nan. 'She's very much into herbs and unguents and things.'

'Is she? Then I'll have a crack at her after lunch. But not now. I'm positively starving and neither man nor doctor can function on an empty stomach.' He kissed her nose again.

Well, it was a kiss of sorts, thought Nan, leading the way into her sitting room where the gateleg table was laid for lunch in the window embrasure. She would have liked something more substantial, more meaningful, but...

'This is nice,' said Callum, waving his hand toward the window and the village lying below. It had begun to snow again, large fluffy flakes that whirled lightly down and settled on ledges and leafless branches and the rooftops below, as well as on the already frozen snow. 'It's years since I've experienced a white Christmas, and now here I am, spending it with you...'

Their eyes met and held and the air seemed to crackle between them.

Nan was elated, scared, bold all at the same time, and a deep, painful longing to turn back the clock and start all over again consumed her. Please, God, let it happen, she prayed, clenching her hands at her sides.

'I'll fetch the pudding,' she said breathlessly, and bolted into the kitchen.

And here she was in the kitchen again. For a moment she looked round, dazed. What was she supposed to be doing? Pudding, that's right, fetching the pudding. They had eaten their soup, the onion soup which had set off sad memories for Callum, if his face had been anything to go by. She knew so little of him really, fragmented snips of information gathered, dropped over the months they'd been together, but she'd had the impression of a happy childhood.

He was sitting as still as a statue, staring out of the window, when she took in the pudding. That was something that had changed about him, she realised, setting the plates and a dish on the table. Stillness. In the past he'd seldom been still.

'Cinnamon and apple tart,' she said brightly, 'with cream. A million calories a mouthful, but necessary in weather like this, especially if you get called out. Anyway, Betty thinks you need building up.'

Callum turned his head slowly, and with relief Nan saw that his face looked less tortured...and his eyes were smiling again. He looked down at his plate. 'Fattening up, more like...' he chuckled '...for Christmas dinner. Betty's a marvellous cook, but she's using me as a guinea pig. Try this, she says, and pops something tasty into my mouth whenever I go near the kitchen. Between her and your Aunt Janet...' he pulled a clownish face '...my poor arteries are going to get totally clogged up.'

Nan's heart turned over and over—she'd always loved the droll faces he'd pulled for the children, especially in the oncology ward. It touched her to the centre of her being to see their small faces, often topped with fine, scanty hair, light up in response.

She sat down opposite him. 'Speaking of Aunt Janet,' she said, 'she's visiting Dr H. and keeping Mrs H. company, so I think I'll be saved an in-depth confrontation with her which I was dreading.' She spooned clotted cream onto her tart. 'I don't know what you told her, but you've certainly retrieved your reputation. She thinks the older version of Dr Callum Mackintosh a definite improvement on the younger one of ten years ago.'

'It needed improving,' Callum said drily. He sampled the apple tart and groaned in appreciation. 'I'll never be able to work this afternoon.'

'You don't have to,' she assured him, 'unless you're called out or there's an emergency. All's well here and Reception will let us know if either of us is needed. So what have you said to bewitch Aunt Janet?'

He took another mouthful of tart, munched it with evident appreciation and then shook his head. 'Nothing definitive. We talked about what I'd been doing since you and I split up and why I'd come to Cornwall.'

Nan pounced. 'And why *have* you come to Cornwall? Your parents live on a Scottish island, your siblings are scattered all around the world, so why here, Callum?' Her pulses raced as she spoke. Had he come looking for her after all these years, or was it a pure accident?

Callum looked at her so long in silence that she thought he was going to refuse to answer.

There was something about the expression on his face that made her speak gently. 'Come on, Callum, love, what brought you to Cornwall and subsequently to Tintore?'

His lip curled at one corner in a familiar fashion. 'You might call it an ironic twist of fate,' he said. 'My parents moved down to the Scilly Isles a few months ago, hoping that the milder climate would help Dad's bronchitis and emphysema. The mainland would have been better, but they're islanders to the core. The move hasn't helped. In fact, he's going downhill fast and I decided to come to work here for the forseeable future, be around to help, you know.'

Nan knew only too well. So that was the irony. He'd come to Cornwall for the same reason that she had ten years ago, to be near a sick relative, in this case his dad who was desperately ill, just as she had come to be with Aunt Janet. But what was he doing here now? Surely he should be in Scilly with his parents for Christmas?

'So why aren't you over there with your parents right now?'

'All the air and sea ferries are booked solid till after New Year. There's nothing even for private hire. But Mum and Dad won't be alone. My brother Alan and sister Moira are with them for the holiday. I shall go over for a few days in January before I start work with the ambulance service here. By then my Australian air doctor qualifications should be cleared. I'm on a part-time contract and will be able to pop over often and be around if Dad needs special care.'

It didn't seem possible that this was the same ambitious man who'd put career above all else. Nan said softly, 'I'm glad you're here for them, Callum. If there's anything I can do to help... We could nurse your father here if he becomes too much for your mother and he could have regular physio...'

Her lovely green eyes were full of sincerity, the real nurse in her longing to help.

Callum got up and strode round the table. He dropped to his knees beside her chair, slid his arms round her waist and kissed her cheek. 'My lovely, generous Nan,' he murmured. 'Oh, my dear, finding you here in Tintore was a beautiful, unexpected, magic bonus that I hadn't imagined in my wildest dreams.' He tugged her gently round to face him.

'But you knew Aunt Janet lived in Tintore, or had you forgotten?' She searched his lightly tanned face so close to hers, noting that the laughter lines were deeper than they used to be—because he'd got into the habit of screwing up his eyes against the glare of the fierce Australian sun or because he was laughing more?

'Nan.' His voice was heavy and serious. 'Believe me, I have forgotten nothing about you, but I was sure that Aunt Janet had died and you had moved on. I just hoped that, by taking up this emergency locum work in the hospital, I could get some news of you. Instead of which, halfway here, Robin dropped his bombshell and I learned that you were Matron.'

He grinned rather shakily. 'I've never fainted in my life, not even on the rugger field, but I came damn near fainting then. Even Robin noticed that I'd changed colour.'

His hands tightened round her waist. 'When I first saw you, recognised you, even though you were muffled up to the eyebrows and blurred by flurries of snow being churned up by the helicopter, I could have shouted—danced—at the sheer joy of seeing you after all these years. And all the time we were loading the stretcher and Dr Latimer onto the plane, my heart felt as if it was going to burst from my body.'

He pressed his lips against her cheek. Nan read it as not so much a love kiss but a kiss of comfort, as if the pressure of his lips would reassure her that his words were sincere. She looked into his eyes. They were brimming with love and tenderness.

Perhaps the time had come to put all her doubts and suspicion behind her, accept that he was a changed man. Aunt Janet obviously had. Nan made up her mind. She slid her hands round his neck and pushed her fingers up through the thick, softly bleached hair nestling at the nape of his neck, as she'd wanted to do since he'd arrived.

'That feels good,' she murmured. 'Your neck feels just the same as it used to, strong and muscular. No, even more muscular, I think.'

Callum gave a throaty chuckle and tilted back his head, squeezing her fingers. 'That'll be all the lumberjacking I did.'

'Lumberjacking! I don't believe it.' Nan slid her hands down onto his shoulders and then down his arms, testing his biceps with her thumbs. Even through his sweater they felt like thick, smooth cord. She smiled and her eyes sparkled. 'Oh, I don't know, though. You always did have good biceps, but now...' She rolled her eyes dramatically.

The phone rang.

They both pulled rueful faces.

Nan dropped her hands from Callum's arms and he stood up. 'Shall I?' He nodded toward the phone sitting on the bureau.

'Please. It's probably for you.'

'That was Marge,' said Callum, as he put down the receiver. 'Glenda Woods has been brought in by the owners of the neighbouring farm. They're in the day unit. Joyce is with them. Apparently her neighbours found her collapsed on the kitchen floor when they went visiting. They sensibly wrapped her in blankets and brought her down in their Land Rover rather than wait for the ambulance to get to them. She's in a lot of pain—not surprising, the state her feet are in. The first thing I want to do is to get some painkillers into her.'

He strode through to the hall and automatically picked up his case, even though the day unit was well equipped. Nan followed him.

'I know Joyce is there, but another pair of hands will be useful, getting Glenda sorted out. She's still likely to resist being admitted, you know, in spite of having collapsed.' She spoke to the top of his shining white gold head as they went down the stairs.

Callum turned to grin up at her. 'This place is teeming with determined, resourceful women but, you know me, I like a challenge.'

'Hmm, especially a female one,' murmured Nan.

Joyce was taking Glenda's blood pressure when they arrived in the surgical room. Callum moved across to stand behind her where he could read the column of fluid going up and down the sphygmomanometer. Nan stopped to speak to the Bennetts, who were standing just inside the door.

'Low,' Joyce said softly over her shoulder to Callum, 'but five minutes ago it was high.'

Callum nodded. 'Typical of Raynaud's,' he said, 'as the arteries contract and relax.' He crouched down beside Glenda who was still in the wheelchair. 'Glenda, can you hear me?'

'Course I can,' muttered Glenda irritably. 'Nothing wrong with my hearing. I only had a bit of a pain in my foot, suddenish. That's what made me fall.' She jerked her thumb towards the Bennetts. 'They panicked. They should have hauled me up and sat me in a chair and I'd have been fine.'

'You wouldn't, you know,' said Callum. 'You'd

probably have died if they'd left you there. Plenty of people die of cold in weather like this, but you, suffering from Raynaud's, are an easy victim. I warned you this morning that you could lose your toes. Well, I'm repeating that warning. If you don't come into hospital and have high-powered care, you might lose more than your toes and you'll be in agony, and I do mean agony. A fat lot of good you'll be to your husband and the farm then.'

His deliberately impatient tone reached Nan and the Bennetts.

'But the stock,' wavered Glenda, her face taut and grey with pain.

Ned Bennett crossed the room and looked down at Glenda. 'You silly old besom,' he said. 'Freda and I will look after the stock and the other beasties, your dogs and hens. It's no problem. Why the devil didn't you let us know that Bob hadn't got back before The Lane got blocked off?'

'I didn't want to be a nuisance,' murmured Glenda, and with a spurt of defiance, 'And not so much of the old.'

Ned snorted. 'What d'ya think friends are for? Bob asked us to keep an eye on you, though he thought he was only going to be away a couple of nights.'

Freda Bennett came across and took Glenda's hand. 'Your Bob would kill us if we let anything happen to you, Glen, and we owe you a favour. You two took care of our place when we had to go up to our Ruth's last summer. Besides, isn't it better to have a few days here in the Cottage, being looked after by Matron Winters and Joyce and the other people you know, rather than having to spend weeks in Truro where they're all strangers?'

Glenda's lips tightened as she bit back a moan of pain, and she slumped in the chair. 'I guess you're right,' she muttered. 'Thanks for everything, Freda, Ned. Don't hang around, it'll be dark soon. Oh, one other thing. Please, leave a message on the answering machine for Bob—tell him where I am but make it as casual as you can.' She looked up at Callum. 'OK, Doctor, I'm all yours. Do what you've got to.'

The Bennetts left and Callum gave Glenda an injection of pethidine before they moved her up to the eight-bedded Edith Cavell ward on the first floor. Only five of the beds were occupied.

Woozy as she was from the quick-acting drug, Glenda recognised the other patients. They'd all lived in Tintore for most of their lives and she'd been at school with two of them. They were all eager to know what she was doing in hospital, and Nan had to warn them to lay off the questioning for the time being, explaining that Glenda wasn't up to socialising at present.

Making Glenda comfortable was much the same as it had been for old Henry, requiring real nursing and that special touch. A glucose drip was set up, through which further painkillers and antibiotics could be introduced. A cradle was placed over her feet, to keep the weight of the bedclothes off her badly wounded toes, and a lightweight warming blanket over her stomach and knees.

She would be looked after by Joan Weatherall, the sister who supervised both the short-term female and adjacent male ward, Logan, named after a long-dead physician who had been the village doctor in 1900.

Sister Joan was a bright, breezy redhead, with a scrap of lace like Nan's perched on a riot of curls.

Callum had met her and two of the auxiliaries, Mavis Long and Carrie Davis, the previous day when Nan had whisked him round on his tour.

They were a cheerful trio and also pretty, guaranteed, Callum thought, to lift anyone's spirits. As a bonus, they all had nice legs, enhanced by the uniform black stockings that used to be the norm. It was years since he'd seen so many neat uniforms, caps and black silk-stockinged legs. Pity they'd gone out of fashion. Clearly the hotchpotch of uniforms often being worn in many large hospitals hadn't yet reached Tintore Cottage Hospital.

This small hospital, tucked away in a remote Cornish village, certainly seemed to attract some talent, starting at the top with a stunning matron. He looked up from the chart he was filling in as the thought flitted through his mind and he met Nan's lovely green eyes. He could see that she knew exactly what he was thinking—she used to tease him about being a leg man.

He gave her a whimsical wink which said as clearly as if he had spoken, okay, so you've caught me out drooling over the opposition's legs—that's something that hasn't changed. He looked down at his chart again. *If and when*, he told himself, *the opportunity arises, I shall take great pleasure in telling her that hers are still the most georgeous legs in the business.*

Her legs had been the first part of her anatomy that he'd seen all those years ago, as she'd done an internal on the sixteen-year-old girl, Lucy. Her head had been hidden beneath the tented sheet draped over Lucy's legs, and only her neat bottom and legs had been visible. He'd never forgotten the girl's name—after all, it had been she who'd brought them together.

Such a vivid poignant memory. He stared unseeingly at the chart, his pen poised above it...

'Doctor, do you want me to change the dressings tonight, or shall I leave them till tomorrow since you did them this morning?' Sister Joan was asking in a voice which said that this was the second time of asking.

He heard Nan give a little snort of amusement as he snapped back to the present, managing to convey the impression that he had been deep in thought about his patient. No way had she been deceived. He avoided her eyes and concentrated on Joan.

'Yes, I've been wondering about that, Sister.' He tapped his teeth with his pen. They gleamed whitely against his tan. 'I think we'd better leave these dressings *in situ.* There's no seepage and Glenda seems comfortable for the moment.' He smiled down at Glenda—she was almost asleep.

'More comfortable than I've been for days,' she mumbled. 'And I'm warm at last.'

Callum put a hand on her shoulder. 'Then we'll leave you to sleep,' he said gently.

He and Nan left the cubicle, leaving Joyce and Joan to put the finishing touches to making Glenda comfortable.

They stood side by side outside Edith Cavell Ward, their hands not quite touching but electrical vibes prickling between them. Nan was so aware of him that she felt herself quivering.

'That's how I feel,' murmured Callum, casting a discreet glance at the nurses' station a few yards away. 'A mass of receptors. If that call hadn't come through...' He let his voice trail off.

Nan turned so that her back was to the station. 'As

Aunt Janet would say, "if" is the smallest, biggest word in the language,' she said softly. She closed her eyes for a moment, depriving Callum of their brilliance, hiding the love that she knew burned in them. She clenched her fists. He'd been back in her life just over twenty-four hours, and look what he had done to her. It was lunacy. She should be doing her best to deflect it, but she couldn't.

His voice was a sibilant whisper. 'Don't fight it, Nan, this was meant to be. We've got a second chance, second time around. Let's think of it as a Christmas miracle. And talking of miracles, I think it's time we showed ourselves in Tiddlywinks. We promised to help with the last of the decorations, remember?'

On the way up to Tiddlywinks, they called in on Dr Horton. He was sleeping peacefully, though his chest was rattling.

Eve was with him, holding an oxygen mask over his mouth and nose.

'I've persuaded Mrs H. and the old matron to go along to the sitting room and have a cup of tea,' she said, 'but I don't think I'll be able to persuade Mrs H. to go home for the night.' She looked at Nan. 'Would it be possible to put up a bed for her here, Matron? There's plenty of room.'

'I'll send Tom along to see to it,' Nan promised immediately.

Callum was examining the obs chart. He nodded with satisfaction. 'Making progress,' he said, 'slowly but surely. It's good to see these small improvements.' He smiled at Eve. 'Keep up the good work, Eve. I'll pop in and see him again this evening—what time do you go off duty?'

Eve looked at Nan. 'I'm not sure,' she said. 'Whenever Matron can get special night cover. I won't go till I have someone to hand over to.'

'Marge is trying to get hold of Belle Carpenter,' Nan replied. 'If we can't get her, we'll try for Molly Short.'

'But Molly's nearly due,' Eve said.

'Not for three weeks,' said Nan, 'and she's fed up to the back teeth just waiting for things to happen, especially with Russell away and knowing that he can't get back till The Lane opens up. It's not physically demanding and Sister Helen will send someone in to do the turning. After all, if you think about it, it's better for her to be here.' She grinned and her green eyes sparkled. 'She's booked for one of our maternity beds and, who knows, perhaps we're going to have a Christmas Eve baby…?'

'*And* she's opted for an epidural,' said Eve. 'How are we going to get hold of an anaesthetist over Christmas, even if he or she is willing to be flown in?'

Nan beamed at her and put a hand on Callum's arm. She was thrilled to feel him tighten his muscles in response. 'So, not everything's got through on the local grapevine. Meet our own in-house anaesthetist. I can vouch for him being a wizard at giving epidurals.'

Eve's mouth fell open. 'Well, I never. Oh, that's brilliant. It means—'

'That if Molly goes into labour over Christmas, we're self-sufficient, and *that* is how I like us to be.'

Don't, thought Nan, watching Callum's face, remind us that you won't be here long. Don't spoil our

Christmas, *my* Christmas. The message had been received.

He gave one of his little half-bows and metaphorically doffed a cavalier's feathered hat. 'We aim to please, ladies,' he said in his soft Sean Connery drawl.

Eve grinned. 'You don't miss a trick, do you, Doctor?'

He chuckled. 'Not if I can help it, with all you smart ladies around.' He looked at his watch. 'Come on, Nan, let's be off to Tiddlywinks and see what they've laid on for us today.'

It was balloons, dozens of them in all the colours of the rainbow. They waded through them ankle-deep in their journey from the door.

'The children have been pumping them up all afternoon,' said a dimpling Polly. 'Now we want someone to put them up—that's right, kids, isn't it?'

'Yeah.' A battery of big, hopeful eyes turned to Callum. He held up his hands. 'OK, I give in. Just point me towards a ladder, and we're in business.'

There was a ladder in the cleaning cupboard.

'And tinsel,' called out Marie. 'Dr Hugh always puts tinsel between each bunch.'

'My word, she's certainly improved since this morning,' said Nan. 'Is it really down to the pain-relief booster?'

'That and a gentle massage with some aromatherapy oils.'

Nan's eyebrows shot up. 'But I told you, there aren't any aromatherapists in the village. I'd have known if there were.'

Callum was busy tying together a bunch of balloons. Under cover of the children's loud chatter, he said, 'But there is at the moment. Polly's friend, who's staying with her, is qualified. She's a bit older than Polly. They met at the nursery nurse training school, so I'm sure she's to be trusted. She was visiting when I popped in this morning. I was intrigued at how good she was with the kids and learned her history. It sounded almost too good to be true, but I sounded her out and she certainly knows her stuff so I asked her to come back this afternoon and give Marie a short session.'

Nan's face was a picture as several emotions chased across it—amazement, bafflement, anger, relief.

Callum's heart dropped like a stone. I've blown it, he thought. I should have asked Nan first. It's her hospital, she's the queen bee—has been for years. She's a constant factor. Patients and staff look to her for guidance. It just seemed the right thing to do for little Marie and I thought Nan would be pleased that we could do something for her pronto. And it was the right thing to do, he assured himself. Patients came first, hurt feelings second, even when they were Nan's.

He began to climb the ladder with an enormous bunch of balloons in one hand and all the children, except Marie, jostling at its foot. The ladder rocked. Looking down, he said wryly to Nan, 'Unless you want your locum to end up with a fractured femur beside your Dr Latimer in Truro General, you'd better steady this thing.'

Nan stared up into his tanned face and laughing eyes as he peered down at her between the multicoloured balloons.

Automatically she put out her hands and steadied the ladder.

Her thoughts raced, veering in one direction and then another. Was he really trying to take over *her* hospital, going above her head without consulting with her, sure that he'd already softened her up? There'd always been a touch of arrogance about him, but it had been bearable because he'd recognised and applauded her desire to get to the top. He'd never tried to dominate her.

She'd seen his charisma at work a dozen times in the past, when he'd talked round some of stuffiest and most rigid ward sisters to get his own way and she'd thought it clever and amusing. After all, it had always been in the interests of the patients and, she had to admit, sometimes to cut a bit of a dash in front of his superiors.

Well, there were no superiors for him to impress here, except herself she acknowledged with a smile, and he's done that all right.

A cheer went up from the children as he fixed the bobbing colourful bunch of balloons in the corner.

'Now the tinsel,' called Marie, throwing a glittering streamer towards Nan.

Nan caught it with one hand and stretched up to pass it to Callum.

'Am I forgiven?' he murmured, as their hands touched.

She slipped a strand of tinsel round his wrist and tugged it gently. 'Nothing to forgive,' she murmured back. 'You did the right thing for the right reasons and I love you for it.'

'Hallelujah, that's all I need to hear,' he said. 'This is going to be the best Christmas in ten long years.'

CHAPTER SEVEN

TEN long years—well, the first five had been long and hard and then her job and responsibilities and being needed had absorbed her. Knowing herself to be loved and respected by this tight-knit community, it had gradually eased the ache in her heart and Nan had learned how to be happy again.

She'd never forgotten Callum and those few months of dizzy happiness with her good-looking, single-minded Scot with the lovely smile and hard core and throaty deep burr. Even in the later years she had sometimes woken with a start and fancied she'd heard his voice murmuring all sorts of silly love nothings in her ear, felt his arms steal round her and hold her close to his warm, naked body, teasing her with his hands and tongue till she turned and they made hot sexy love...

Young Peter stumbled into her, his hard plaster ankle cast grazing her ankle and jerking her into the present.

She pulled a mock cross face. 'Hey, Pete, do you mind?' She shifted her leg.

Peter said ruefully, 'I'm sorry, Matron. I'm not very good with this yet, but I'll be fine by Christmas—promise.'

Nan grinned. 'Bet you'll be in goal for the junior Tintore Rovers by the end of the season.'

His face lit up. 'Wow,' he said.

Callum was still busy fighting with the balloons,

getting them into some sort of order and muttering under his breath, but there was a smile on his face as broad as young Peter's. There was no doubting that he was happy.

Nan felt warmed through and through by the words he'd spoken, endorsed by his dazzling, laughing hazel eyes. Looking up at him, balancing on one leg on the top step of the ladder as he reached up and sideways, her heart felt fit to burst. She liked this new, mature version of the younger Callum.

She didn't know what was going to happen after Christmas, whether he would go away and simply disappear into the blue once the crisis with his father was over—not that he'd said anything to indicate that he would, but at this moment it was enough that they were joined by a bond of loving memories.

Memories that might be turned into something more substantial. Callum had seemed to hint—no, more than hint—at the idea. What had he said about a second time around? Would it be possible? Could they begin again, turn back the clock? Older and wiser, start with a clean slate? Her already full heart pounded at the thought.

Callum fastened one end of a length of tinsel beneath the bunch of balloons and began to descend the ladder. Nan continued to steady it in a death grip. In truth, she seemed unable to prise her fingers loose.

He reached the bottom of the ladder and bent to whisper in her ear, 'I'm down now, love, you can let go.'

It took a moment for his words to penetrate and then it was his warm breath trailing across her sensitive earlobe that reached her before she interpreted his words. She blushed and released her hold, though she seemed glued to the spot and couldn't move her feet. Dear God, was she so obvious?

The children were rolling and chasing around, collecting balloons from the floor to take to Polly who was tying them up into bunches. The level of noise was extraordinary, considering these were eight sick children.

Taking advantage of the children's preoccupation with the balloons, not even checking to see if he was observed, Callum kissed Nan on the mouth and rubbed his nose to hers, slowly and sensually. It was an old caress, used instead of words to say sorry when they'd had disagreements—few and far between in the early months of their loving, more frequent in the latter weeks before they'd parted when disagreements had become full-blown bitter rows.

'Oh, my dear,' he murmured, 'how could we have let things get out of hand? How could I have said the things that I did?' He took a tendril of tawny hair that curled against her forehead between his finger and thumb, pulled it gently and let it spring back into place. 'I'm so looking forward to seeing it unpinned and cascading in a rippling mass, as the romantics would have it, down to…your shoulders, or perhaps shoulder blades…?'

Nan dimpled and smiled and fluttered her long lashes at him, she couldn't help herself. She wanted to flirt with him as she'd done in those long ago, fancy-free days. 'Give or take an inch or two either way,' she said, as he'd done regarding his height.

At the moment, she guessed, her hair would be down to her shoulder blades. It had been weeks since she'd had it cut, and it grew furiously, becoming a cloud of fine curls when she released it at night. The thought of displaying it to Callum, and perhaps have him stroke it...brush it...his strong, capable hands wielding the brush firmly as he got it under control, sent her off again, daydreaming.

She mustn't do it. Emotionally, she was going up and down like a yo-yo and she shouldn't be, not at her age. She put a hand over her heart to still its wild beating, for all the world like a shy Victorian lady.

Callum didn't miss the gesture. 'This love thing,' he whispered, 'is painful, is it not?'

'Yes,' she whispered back, 'painful and exciting and unpredictable... What are we going to do, Callum?'

He blinked at the brilliance of her eyes. He'd never seen them look so sexy and yet they held, too, a kind of innocence—the way she wanted him to decide was very appealing. This strange mixture of strength and helpless femininity had always intrigued him. The combination was powerful and it still intrigued him.

He cleared his throat. 'I know what I want to do, but...' He looked down as young Wendy tugged at his trousers.

'Polly says that you've got to put the next bunch up, Dr Mac,' she said firmly. 'And don't forget to put the tinsel up, too.'

'No ma'am,' he said, sketching a salute, and then murmured quietly into Nan's ear, 'I seem to have my instructions. Look, Nan, you go and do whatever you have to do—rounds or something—and I'll come up to the flat in an hour or so. I can't bear being so close to you and not...well, you get the message.'

'I do.' She chuckled, her eyes greener and sexier than ever. 'Where's this doctor who likes a female challenge, then?'

Another theatrical groan. 'Lost when it comes in batches of charmers covering all ages,' he said, laying a hand on Wendy's head.

It was a tender gesture and for a fleeting moment Nan had a vision of him as he might have been with a child of his own. Callum the tough career-man with a child of his own—what nonsense! She scrubbed the mental picture, waved goodbye to Polly and the kids and walked briskly out into the corridor.

She did a round, not because Callum had suggested it but because she tried to fit in an afternoon round when she could. There were usually a fair number of visitors about at this time of day, many itching to have a few words with her about their relatives' progress.

Some already knew that their husband, wife, son, daughter or whoever would be home for the holiday and wanted to confirm what time they could be collected on the following day, Christmas Eve. Some would have to wait till Callum did his round tomorrow to know if their loved one would be home by Christmas Day. All of them were full of praise for the care that had been given, and had brought Nan and her staff brightly coloured thank-you packages, to be placed under the tree in Reception.

It was the same every year and Nan never ceased to be moved by their generosity.

Everyone she spoke to praised the decorations in the wards and corridors, a combined effort by Dave and ward staff. Nan, walking along the first-floor corridor, thought that Dave had surpassed himself this year. His theme was silver and gold tinsel interspersed with snow-sprayed greenery and fake hanging icicles. The theme was repeated in the downstairs corridors.

Quite suddenly, for no apparent reason, she felt incredibly weary, almost tearful and desperately in need of a cup of strong tea. The ups and downs of the day had got to her.

She crossed Reception with a smile and a nod for everyone and leaned across the front desk. 'Marge, I'll be in the kitchens if I'm wanted. I need a stiff cuppa.'

The cook, Betty, took one look at her, pushed her onto a stool and slapped a mug of tea in front of her on the worktop. Then she placed a plate of freshly baked macaroons in front of her.

'Drink, eat,' she said, pointing to the mug and plate. She poured tea for herself and sat down beside Nan. She examined Nan's face thoughtfully. 'You look…not exactly tired, Matron, but as if you've got a load of problems to be resolved and no time to sort them. I can almost hear the wheels turning. You work too hard and too long every day.'

Nan laughed loudly. 'That's the pot calling the kettle black,' she said.

'Ah, but I don't have your responsibilities and I've a good crowd of girls helping me.' She took a mouthful of tea and jerked her head towards the preparation kitchen. She smiled indulgently. 'Hark at them, always having a laugh, that lot. They're getting the veg ready for supper and a couple of them are staying on to help with the baking for the carol service tomorrow.'

Nan was already feeling better. Her sudden down mood had lifted. Sipping her tea, dunking Betty's delicious macaroons and listening to Betty's lovely local slow drawl, as thick as Cornish cream, she began to relax. The kitchen, though clinically tiled white, was homely. The large Aga purring softly, with aromatic foody smells coming from it, the subdued laughter from the next-door kitchen... It was like a warm cocoon, a sanctuary, thought Nan... And if I don't get up soon I'll fall asleep.

She swallowed the last of her tea and stood up. 'Betty...' Her voice was husky. 'Thanks for everything you do, for running the kitchens like a dream, so that I never have to worry about them. You're a gem.' Hesitantly, she touched Betty's sturdy forearm. 'I don't want to embarrass you, but you should know that I couldn't—the hospital couldn't—manage without you. You're much appreciated and I wouldn't have your job for anything.'

Betty went red. She grinned shyly. 'Oh, get away with you, Matron. No one's indispensable. And I certainly wouldn't have your job, masterminding everything, always on call night and day.'

The wallphone shrilled and she lifted the receiver off the hook. She listened for a moment and handed the receiver to Nan. 'It's Marge for you, Matron. One of the Lawson boys has been brought in with a nasty cut.'

Nan's heart sank as she took the phone. It would be one of the nine-year-old Lawson twins, who between them could have put forward a good case for keeping a cottage hospital open in Tintore.

'Bobby or Kit?' she asked, 'and how badly cut? Please, tell me it's Bobby.' Bobby's blood clotted normally. Kit wasn't classed as an haemophiliac, but had a slow clotting time and bled like a stuck pig from even a small wound.

'It's Bobby,' confirmed Marge, 'but Joyce says it's a deep cut across the inside of his forearm. She's working on it but needs help. The boys were chopping wood.'

Nan groaned. 'Of course they were,' said Nan drily. 'What else? I'll be with her stat. Have you notified Callum? He's with the kids.'

'He's finished there and has gone down to the village stores—on a shopping spree, he said.'

Her mind boggled. Gone down to the stores on a shopping spree—what for, for heaven's sake? None of your business, she reminded herself.

'OK,' she said. 'You might have to get him back up here. I'll look at Bobby's arm and see if we're going to need his services. It may be something Joyce and I can deal with without his help, but we'd better be prepared.'

She sped through to the day unit.

She and Joyce inspected Bobby's arm. The blood kept welling up in spite of the tourniquet and the fact that Kit was holding Bobby's arm up as instructed by Joyce. It would need some clever stitching. If pressed, they would have tackled the job as they had so often in the past, suturing the wound superficially before shipping him out to Truro for further treatment under anaesthetic.

Truro, however, was almost a no-no. With the weather worsening, the air ambulance was under terrific pressure. Yet this was a dreadfully long diagonal wound, running from the inside of the boy's elbow almost to his wrist. It was also deep in places and needed expert attention. It was the depth of the cut in places that bothered Nan.

'I think we could have nerve and muscle and possibly blood-vessel damage here, Joyce, don't you agree?'

Joyce nodded. 'And some deep-layer clever stitching is a must if the lad's not going to lose partial use of hand and arm.'

She kept her voice low, but Bobby and his twin, both already pale, looked paler.

Bobby spoke to Nan, his voice fearful. 'What d'ya mean, Matron—lose the use of my hand?'

'Bobby, love, don't panic. That's not likely to happen. I'll explain in a minute,' Nan said. 'Joyce, get Marge to get hold of Doctor Mac, stat—and let's have another nurse in here.'

Joyce was at the phone before she'd finished speaking.

Nan slowly released the above-elbow tourniquet on the boy's elevated arm, but kept the pressure pad directly over the wound in place. 'Keep his arm up,' she directed Kit, as blood seeped through the pressure bandage. Seeing his scared look, she added, 'I'll put the tourniquet back in a moment, but I want to make sure that his circulation to his fingertips is OK.'

'Understood,' replied Kit through stiff lips, more anxious on his brother's behalf than he usually was when he himself was injured.

Nan felt the tips of Bobby's fingers and nodded. 'They're fine,' she said. 'You're a tough pair.' She began to refix the tourniquet.

Her remark had the desired effect and both lads produced shaky grins.

Joyce came off the phone and a few minutes later one of the auxiliaries, Jenny Benson, was standing in the doorway, hands on hips, tut-tutting and shaking her head.

'Might have known it was one of you two,' she

said, the grumble in her voice belied by a sympathetic grin. 'I suppose you expect me to clear up this mess.'

They all looked at the blood and dirty snow on the floor and the couch, the boys sheepishly, Nan and Joyce hiding a twinkle in their eyes. This was exactly the tone and manner to adopt with the twins, who could be difficult if they had a mind to be. But Jenny had known them since they were babies and knew exactly how to deal with them.

They lived in the next-door cottage to her, near the foot of the hospital drive, and she'd often babysat them as their mother was widowed and had to go out to work.

She would be working now and would have to be informed.

'Before you start clearing up, Jenny, will you give Grace a ring at the hairdresser's and let her know what's happened? Use the phone in Reception. Tell her not to panic, everything's in hand, but if she could get away...' Her eyes told Jenny what her words did not, that there was some urgency for her to come. She wasn't sure what Callum would decide to do, but Grace would need to know about it and perhaps give her consent to treatment.

Callum had worked for over two hours, repairing Bobby's arm, and that had been after he'd sedated the child as much as he'd dared.

'Ideally, this should be done under a general,' he'd explained to Grace before he'd begun. 'But I've done this sort of repair before, putting the patient under sedation and freezing the limb as much as possible.' He'd touched Grace's hand. 'Bobby's willing for me to have a go—will you trust your son to my surgical skills?'

Grace had nodded, her eyes signalling her consent before she'd voiced it. 'Go ahead Doctor, I've every faith in you. Matron has assured me that you're a brilliant doctor and I value her judgement.'

Callum had said gently, with a twinkle in his eyes, 'Then, if Matron's given the thumbs-up, let's get cracking.'

They moved Bobby into the day-surgery room, which Joyce and Jenny had transformed into a mini-theatre. Whilst Jenny took care of Grace and Kit in the office, plying them with tea, Coke and biscuits, Nan and Joyce assisted Callum with the complicated piece of surgery to be performed.

Joyce acted as theatre sister, anticipating Callum's needs, handing him instruments before he asked for them. Nan assisted him, aspirating blood out of the wound so that he could see what he was doing.

She held retractors and forceps in position as he connected blood vessels and tiny nerve endings, an incredibly intricate job. And when he began stitching, the deep layers first, with soluble thread that would dissolve in time, she swabbed and filled the wound with antibiotic powder.

At last he reached the final stage, the superficial skin stitching, and she snipped off the ends of thread and covered the wound with Melolin and a thick pad of gauze. That done, she and Joyce, under Callum's supervision, positioned Bobby's forearm on a support foam board. Leaving his fingers exposed for observation, they bandaged it neatly in place from palm to elbow, finally supporting his arm in a sling.

Callum tore off his gloves, chucked them in the bin

and produced one of his dazzling smiles. Then he inclined his head and said in his Sean Connery voice, 'Thank you for your help, ladies. Good teamwork.' He sounded for all the world like a surgeon in a proper theatre.

The best surgeons always remembered to thank their staff, Nan thought.

That had been several hours ago, Nan realised as she unlocked the door of her flat and stood back to let Callum through into the hall.

He shook his head. 'You first,' he said, giving her a little push.

Too tired to argue, Nan went through to the sitting room, switching on lights as she went. She made a beeline for the drinks cupboard.

'Whisky or brandy? You can relax now, Callum. Night staff have taken over—two senior experienced night sisters, utterly reliable, and a full complement of staff nurses and auxiliaries. Both Dr Horton and young Bobby are being specialled—'

Callum interjected, 'I hope that your pregnant young woman isn't specialling Dr H. I should have mentioned it earlier—not a good idea three weeks to term to nurse an infectious patient.'

Nan flushed and looked uncomfortable. She said drily. 'Of course it isn't. I don't know what made me suggest her…' She did. Callum's presence had sent everything out of her head and she'd wanted to show him off, surprise everyone with the knowledge that he was an anaesthetist and could deal with an epidural. What she'd really had in mind had been for Molly to relieve another nurse who could then have specialled the doctor. Such childish nonsense. It was ridiculous and she was thoroughly ashamed of herself.

Her flush deepened. 'I came to my senses, talked it over with Joyce and we came up with a contingency plan if Belle Carpenter couldn't do it. In the event, she could, and she's specialling Dr H. until the morning, so Helen Bright has been able to send one of her regular night nurses to special young Bobby. Which means, as I said, that you can relax and have a drink.'

She glanced over her shoulder. 'So, what is it to be?'

Callum didn't answer at once. He was lounging on the sofa, his legs stretched out in front of him, ankles crossed, hands linked behind his head, eyes half-closed. Nan couldn't even be sure that he was looking at her, or even awake. There was just a gleam between almost closed, long lashed lids.

She had an uncanny feeling that he'd seen through her and said quickly, 'You can stay in the spare staff bedroom along the corridor first on the left, so there's no problem about getting back to Aunt Janet's. And there's a plate of succulent sandwiches in the fridge to soak up the alcohol, courtesy of Betty.'

'Hmm, yum, Betty, the culinary queen of the cottage hospital,' he said, sinking lower into the squashy depths of the sofa and thrusting his legs out nearer the wood-effect gas fire with its almost realistic flickering glow. 'I'm ravenous—and it'll be a whisky, please. What full-blooded Scotsman would swap that for a brandy?' He raised one eyebrow. 'I thought you would have remembered that, Nan.'

Of course she'd remembered, but there was no reason why he should know that. She shrugged. 'Your tastes might have changed in all your ramblings about the world.' She poured them both a generous dram and handed him his glass. Kicking off her shoes, with a little grunt of appreciation, she sank down into a large armchair at right angles to the sofa.

She immediately shot up again. 'Sandwiches,' she muttered, and padded towards the kitchen.

She returned a couple of minutes later. 'Napkins but no plates,' she said, plonking the serving dish of sandwiches down on the coffee-table between them.

Callum picked up a sandwich and bit into it. 'Fantastic,' he said, his mouth full.

They ate and drank in silence for a few minutes, then Nan said softly, 'You always were ravenously hungry after doing a tricky job.' She almost added, And after making love.

His eyes met hers. Was he remembering the love bit? 'Yes, I was, wasn't I? Still am, as you can see, but much of me has changed, Nan, important things, the things that matter to you and me.'

Nan held his gaze, her eyes thoughtful. Now that her energy levels had been restored by food and drink, and she'd more or less apologised for suggesting that the pregnant Molly special the doctor, she felt calm, peaceful—and she suddenly discovered that she wanted answers. It was all right for Callum to say that he'd changed, but what had happened to change him, apart from his father's illness?

She glanced at the clock on the mantelpiece—nearly ten. Not as late as she'd thought—they'd crammed so much into the last few hours. He hadn't questioned the arrangements she'd made for him for the night. Had he been expecting, hoping, that he would be staying, but perhaps not in a staff bedroom?

Fair enough, if they hadn't been disturbed after lunch...

'Do you feel up to talking or are you too tired after that magnificent piece of surgery?' she asked abruptly.

He was very alert, his eyes bright. 'My adrenalin's still pumping round at speed. I won't be able to sleep for hours and I want to check our two specials before I turn in. So let's talk, Nan.'

She chose her words carefully, having taken another sip of whisky and curled her feet up under her.

Callum missed her opening remarks. She's so small, he thought, yet so dynamic, the title of dragon suits her very well. I wonder if she remembers the little glass dragon that I bought her in the market? I wonder what's happened to it? I bought it on the day we got engaged, from the same stall that I bought the antique engagement ring. She gave me the ring back, but the little glass dragon...

Her voice broke through his jumbled thoughts. 'So what I want to know is, what *did* you say to Aunt Janet to make you suddenly flavour of the month? She once thought you a total heel to have broken off our engagement. She never did buy my story that it was by mutual consent—not surprising that she guessed, though, the way I walked round like a zombie for months.'

He lifted his head. 'Did you really, Nan? Did you miss me so much?'

His voice sounded tender, yet raw and full of wonder, as if it surprised him that she'd cared so much. How was it possible that they'd lived together for months and he hadn't realised how much she'd loved him? How deeply he'd hurt her when he'd walked out of her life? Oh, she'd been angry, but so had he. He'd expected her to go to America with him, help further his career and be able to further her own. At the time it had seemed so simple—they could both have worked at their careers and been together.

Then Aunt Janet's leukaemia had shattered all that, and he hadn't understood, not then, why Nan had wanted to be with her. By the time it had begun to dawn on him a couple of years later how selfish he'd been, it had been too late and he hadn't known where to look for her.

He stared at her and repeated, 'Did you miss me so much?'

She said softly, 'Yes, I missed you very much, Callum. For a while I didn't think life was worth living. If it hadn't been for Aunt Janet needing me, and then the hospital...'

He looked aghast. 'Nan, you wouldn't have done anything foolish, would you? You're far too—'

'Sensible? Level-headed?'

Callum nodded. 'All that and then some. Oh, Nan, I can't believe that you could have seriously contemplated, well, taking your own life. You've seen too many bodged attempts, for one thing.'

He heaved himself out of the sofa and knelt down beside her shabby armchair so that his face was on a level with hers. 'Oh, my dear, I never meant to hurt you so much. But you always treated this thing that was between us as just chemistry. You seemed to make light of it except for the sex bits.'

'So did you,' she flashed back at him. 'You used to say that it was a good thing that we were both hell bent on a career and wouldn't let anything interfere with that. That all this love stuff wasn't for real—it was just chemistry, hormones.'

He sat back on his heels. 'I did, didn't I?' He ran his fingers again through his thick thatch of sun-bleached hair. 'How wrong can one be? It had nothing to do with that, Nan. I was simply scared stiff of admitting to myself that I was in love with you.'

Nan searched his face with puzzled eyes. 'Yet you wanted me to go with you to the States, even though I wasn't sure that would be the best course for my career. We even went through the charade of getting engaged. If you were that scared of falling in love, wouldn't it have been better to have accepted the job and gone off on your own, made a clean break? Though, of course, your new bosses preferred to employ someone committed on the personal front, didn't they?'

Callum said haltingly, 'Well, more or less, but I wouldn't have got engaged, Nan, had I not loved you, even though I didn't really realise that I was in love with you.'

'But your love didn't extend to supporting me when Aunt Janet fell ill.'

He shook his head. 'No, I panicked. The thought of taking on a sick elderly relative as well as a wife...' He spread his hands in a gesture of regret, despair. 'I was just too damned selfish to do it. I've regretted it every day since—or nearly every day,' he amended. 'It didn't hit me for a while, what I'd done. The work was exciting, I was working all hours, getting some pieces published about anaesthetics. I managed to blot you out of my mind.'

'And is this what you told Aunt Janet?'

'Yes, but I played down the bit about her illness

triggering off the chain of events, though I'm not sure that she was deceived.'

'I doubt it, but you obviously said something that wiped out the past, made her believe in you. What was it, Callum? What convinced an old toughie like Aunt Janet that you're the genuine article?'

'No single thing, but I guess it was when I told her that I'd decided to opt out of the rat race and had turned down an offer to work at Harvard, doing research, in favour of a missionary stint in Africa that she looked at me with a different eye.'

He shifted from one knee to the other and Nan fancied she saw him blushing faintly under his golden tan. 'I didn't say it to impress, but I did want her to know that I'd had a genuine change of heart and wanted to return to the grass roots of medicine. Do hands-on doctoring. That I'd made a dreadful mistake, walking out on you. And, of course, the fact that I was here and was going to be working for the local air ambulance service was pretty convincing.'

Nan looked deep into his hazel eyes, then leaned forward and kissed him on the cheek. 'You'd better get up,' she said, touching him on the shoulder. 'Your knees will be numb. I bet it's a long time since you've done penance on your knees, Callum Mackintosh.'

He nodded. 'Quite a few years.'

Nan's mouth twitched at the corners. 'Let's call it a day on making confessions. I'm absolutely bushed and you must be, too. I just want to say that I'm very, very glad that you've come back into my life, Callum. You're the best Christmas present ever.'

He took her in his arms at the door of the flat. 'I feel I've come home,' he whispered. 'At last.'

CHAPTER EIGHT

NAN closed the door behind Callum and stood leaning against it, supported by the solid wood, breathing heavily, great deep breaths that made her chest rise and fall—like a pouter pigeon, Callum had told her once, or a little robin redbreast on a cold winter's morning.

'Are you saying that I'm fat?' she'd challenged him.

He'd bent over and buried his face between the two soft mounds of her breasts, and had said in a muffled voice, 'I'm saying that you're cuddly and malleable, just as a woman should be. Stick thin may be fashionable, but give me something to hold onto any day.' And he'd slid his hands up beneath her red sweatshirt and minuscule bra and had cupped her breasts with his large, well-shaped hands.

Inevitably they'd ended up in bed, she recalled dreamily. Their sex life had been great. If only the rest of it had matched up. Perhaps it had now, at last.

'I feel I've come home.' That's what Callum had just said.

She closed her eyes and thought of those few minutes in his arms. She could still feel the imprint of his warm hands on her back, holding her close so that they almost melted into each other.

After all these years it still felt familiar, right, to be there in his arms with wave after wave of love flowing between them. They'd joked about it in the past, blamed raging hormones, testosterone and endorphins and any other chemical they could think of, afraid to even say the word 'love' with any meaning. They'd kept the charade up until that day, out of the blue, when Callum had asked her to marry him.

They were in the market and he'd just bought her the fat little glass dragon, all fiery reds, blues and greens. 'Because it reminds me of you,' he'd said. 'With your bright mind and brilliant ideas, sometimes spitting fire over the shortcomings of the health service. Swearing that you'll change things once you get to the top.'

He'd been on a high that day, bubbling over with the thrill and satisfaction of a difficult job well done. In the early hours of the morning, he'd handled the anaesthetising of a woman admitted for an emergency Caesarean for the delivery of twins.

She'd been chesty and had had high blood pressure and had been smoking up to the time of her admission. The babies were premature and undersized. Nobody had been able to track down his boss, the consultant anaesthetist, so Callum had had to work with only a junior to assist.

There was an atmosphere in Theatre, he told Nan later, that absolutely crackled with apprehension. Nobody really thought that all three patients would survive with those sort of odds stacked against them. And the key to keeping them alive to allow the surgeons time to do their job rested with him and the careful administration of the anaesthetic—enough time for them to work, yet as short as possible on account of the woman's condition and the babies' frailty.

'But I did it,' he shouted exuberantly when he got

back to the flat, wrapping his arms round Nan's waist and swinging her off the floor. 'Let's go out and celebrate. Coffee and sticky doughnuts in the market and then I'll buy you something special to remember this day by.'

It was a chilly, breezy day. They walked hand in hand round the market, their faces glowing as the wind bit into their cheeks, their eyes shining with happiness. It was enough that they were together, their futures mapped out for them. It didn't matter what they called this thing between them that sent them flying into each other's arms at the drop of a hat.

And that was when he spotted the little dragon, set out on their favourite stall amongst other ornaments and bracelets and rings and things, where from time to time they'd bought pieces for the flat.

Nan smiled to herself. He wouldn't have given the little dragon a thought since then and would be astonished if she told him it was sitting now where it belonged, on her bedside cabinet.

It had been while the man behind the stall had been carefully wrapping it up that Callum's eye had fallen on the antique ring. Genuine or not, it had been beautiful—a green stone in a silver setting. It had obviously not been an emerald, but it had been a good stone and had had depth and sparkle, like the real thing.

'It matches your eyes,' he'd said, holding it up to eye level. And had then added, without a pause, 'Let's get engaged—marry me, Nan.' He'd added very carefully, spelling it out, *'I love you.'*

No jokes about Cupid's arrow, or across a crowded room, or testosterone rising. Just those three little words and Callum pushing the ring on her finger and the stallholder saying, 'Good on you, mate.'

How long she'd stood there lost in the past, Nan had no idea until the clear tones of the church clock, measuring out midnight, impinged on her senses. It was the twenty-fourth of December, Christmas Eve, and she had a busy, busy day ahead of her, starting with a full round with Callum in the morning, the discharging of patients, the reassuring chats with relatives, the checking that all was in order for the festivities over the next few days.

In the afternoon, she and as many staff, patients and visitors who could manage it would congregate in Tiddlywinks for the children's version of the nativity story. It was always a surprise as they only kept approximately to the plot and that changed at each rehearsal. And the long day would end with the carol-singing. Headed by the choir, everyone would trudge up from the church, bearing candles or lanterns, and sing their hearts out.

Trestle tables would be laid up in the big sitting room, loaded with a Betty-style buffet, out-of-this-world pastries, sherry trifles, wine, cider and soft drinks. It was a marathon effort for all the staff but very worth it. A big family party.

The same routine had been enacted for many years, but this year... With a tired but happy sigh, Nan pushed herself away from the door. Dreamily she went through the motions of bathing, cleaning her teeth and snuggling down under the duvet.

Christmas Eve was always magical and this year, with Callum beside her, was like something out of a fairy story—angels, shepherds, kings, Santa Claus,

Rudolph, the manger and a sleeping babe in swaddling clothes...

Nan woke at six thirty, feeling fresh and rested and bubbling over with joy. 'Joy to the world,' she sang softly. If she'd dreamed, she didn't remember her dream. A faint eerie white light filtered round the edges of the curtains—snowlight.

She showered, coiled her hair up into a gleaming, elaborate French chignon and tucked a small sprig of holly, cut from the bunch in the brass jug in the fireplace, in amongst the coils. For good measure, she touched up the natural light streaks in her tawny tresses from the bottle the hairdresser had given her on her last visit. She put on the merest smudge of soft green eye shadow and a dash of mascara, lip gloss, followed by a quick spray of light perfume. There, all done. She was ready to face the day.

Her newly laundered uniform was lying over the back of a chair. She stood and looked at it for a moment... No, not uniform, not today. Today was a day to celebrate, burst out, proclaim her own joy to the world.

She would wear her black velvet trouser suit and new, red cashmere sweater which Aunt Janet had given her for her birthday. She giggled. It was robin redbreast red. Would Callum remember, get the message, understand that it was an invitation to start all over again, just as he'd said he wanted?

Her wavering was over. Last night had clinched it. Callum, mark two, was a different man to the Callum who'd abandoned her ten years ago. The selfish, hard-driving force of this new man had been remoulded, refined, redirected away from self, outward toward other people. The brilliant doctor of excellence was still there, but he'd added more skills to the one in which he'd excelled.

He was now an all-round, hands-on doctor, which is what he'd been meant to be. There had been flashes of this caring man in the past, but they had been deliberately squashed by his compulsion to get to the top, fast. And the way to do that had been by specialising and sticking to anaesthetics.

The phone shrilled, shattering her mental meanderings. It was Aunt Janet. 'Nan, may I invite myself to breakfast? I'll be up in a few minutes—Callum wants a change of clothes. And then I'm yours for the rest of the day, specialling or wherever you need me.'

Nan put the front door on the latch and, prising her mind away from fantasies of Callum showering and towelling with rivulets of water trickling down his broad chest with its sheen of golden hair, made coffee and a pile of toast. Aunt Janet had a good appetite.

'Cooee, it's only me.' She breezed into the sitting room a short time later. She uncoiled a long scarf and shed a quilted parka. 'I've delivered Callum his clean clothes and invited him to breakfast—didn't think you'd mind.'

Of course she didn't mind, Nan assured her, giving thanks for her forthright aunt as her heart turned cartwheels. She cut some more bread to toast. He'd always been a big breakfast man—was he still? she wondered.

'I gave him porridge and bacon and egg and toast yesterday,' said Janet.

'Tough,' said Nan. 'I haven't got any porridge or bacon. He'll have to make do with scrambled eggs and toast this morning, unless he goes down to the kitchen and asks Betty to feed him.'

'That,' said Janet, 'would be a bad move.'

Nan pulled a face and Janet held up her hands in a gesture of surrender. 'Sorry, interfering.'

'No, you're not,' said Nan. 'You were going to say that I should see as much of him as I can, weren't you, you old witch? And you're right. I've come to that conclusion. We've got to make up for lost time. He's changed, Aunty Janet, hasn't he? You didn't trust him all those years ago, but now…'

'He's a good man, he's worked in some of the grimmest, dirtiest places on earth and has learned a thing or two about people and commitment and compassion. He won't let you down again, Nan.' She spread lashing of butter and marmalade on toast and took a bite.

She crunched for a moment and then said, her mouth half-full, 'Pleased you put your glad rags on. Go and slay him, my girl. That red does things for you—thought it would.'

Callum, when he arrived five minutes later, clearly thought so too. 'Wow!' he exclaimed, much as young Peter crashing around in his plaster had done. 'You look fan*tas*tic. That red is absolutely right for you, brings out the highlights in your hair.' His eyes dropped to her breasts to which the soft cashmere clung as she breathed rapidly in and out. She saw his eyes widen. '*Déjà vu,*' he whispered. 'It's my little robin redbreast.'

They were standing in the hall.

'You remembered!'

'I've never forgotten.'

'Really?'

'Really, and my sentiments haven't changed. I still like my women...'

From the sitting room came the sound of a knife clattering on a plate and a chair being pushed back. They both giggled softly.

'Aunt Janet,' mouthed Nan, 'letting us know she's there and can overhear us.'

They opened the door to the sitting room.

'I've ears like a bat,' said Aunt Jane cheerfully. 'Thought I'd better warn you in case you said something *not* for third-party consumption.'

'Haven't you got any old-age symptoms?' teased Callum. 'Breathlessness, aching limbs, indigestion?'

Aunt Jane shook her head. 'Nope,' she said. 'I'm as fit as a fiddle.' She turned to Nan. 'I'll leave you two lovebirds together. I'll be up with the Hortons. Give me a shout when you want me elsewhere.'

They heard the front door close behind her.

Callum said, 'Lovebirds notwithstanding, I am *not* going to take you in my arms and kiss you silly. If I did, I should have you in bed, making up for ten years' lost loving, and I wouldn't be able to stop.' His eyes danced. 'And I think that after a while someone might become aware of the fact that both matron and locum were missing.'

'And inevitably come up with the right answer,' said Nan with a chuckle, letting her eyes roam over him.

His thick mane of hair was brushed back and he was wearing a bright tartan waistcoat over a green cord shirt and matching cord pants that fitted like jeans. He looked fantastic, very masculine, the tartan waistcoat emphasising the broadness of his torso. Her eyes slid down to his feet, large like his hands, and, like his hands, perfectly formed, though, of course, they were hidden...*in polished brogues*!

Already surprised by the number of clothes he seemed to have crammed into the bulging kitbag he'd brought with him, she positively gaped. On the first day he'd worn the neat combat boots in which he'd arrived, and yesterday soft moccasin-type shoes which might easily have been squashed into a small space. But brogues, good solid brogues?

She was speechless and just pointed.

Callum gave a deep, throaty laugh. 'Courtesy of Aunt Janet,' he said, 'or rather one of her previous lodgers, who apparently left them behind when he departed. Lucky, aren't I? They fit perfectly.' He turned one foot this way and that to show off the gleaming leather.

'Mmm, nice ankles.' Nan grinned, adding, 'Aunt Janet's spoiling you.'

'I know, we're like that.' He crossed his fingers. 'But, seriously, Nan, we've established a marvellous rapport. More than ever I regret not supporting you when she was so desperately ill. She's told me how super you were when she was going through the chemotherapy and how you wouldn't let her give in.'

He frowned, furrows appearing on his broad forehead, his hazel eyes sombre for a moment. 'Oh, my dear, lovely girl.' He took her hands in his and brought them to his lips. 'Don't laugh at me, but I really do want to spend the rest of my life making up to you for beetling off to the US for the sake my precious career. How you must have hated me.'

She didn't want to laugh. She wanted to cry, to give way to all sorts of emotions that she'd been suppressing for years—but most of all she wanted to tell him that she'd long ago stopped hating him for what he'd done.

There was a knock at the door. Fiercely, Callum kissed her fingertips, then dropped her hands and picked up a piece of toast. 'Saved by the bell,' he said softly.

'I love you,' she whispered, and went to answer the door.

Marge was standing outside, staggering under the weight of a large cardboard box. 'The village stores have sent this up for Callum, result of yesterday's shopping spree,' she explained, 'and I don't know where to put it. They say they'll be bringing up another one later.'

She and Nan grinned at each other, both knowing that Marge had used it as an excuse to come up to the flat. Trust Marge, thought Nan, perfect timing. Not ready at the beginning of a busy day to plumb the depths of her feelings for Callum, she was glad of the diversion. Common sense told her that she must keep it light today. They had both expressed their love for each other and at the moment that was enough.

Callum appeared behind Nan. 'Here, I'll take it.' He lifted the box from Marge's arms and strode through to the sitting room.

'Come in and have some coffee,' Nan suggested.

'You sure?' Marge mouthed, her eyes following Callum as he disappeared into the sitting room.

'Positive.'

Nan poured Marge and Callum a coffee and topped up her own. Neither she nor Marge could take their eyes off the large box sitting in the middle of the floor.

It was Callum's turn to grin. 'Curious, ladies?'

'Yes.' They spoke in unison.

His grin widened. He patted the box. 'Then you'll have to contain your curiosity for a few more hours. I need to do a bit of wrapping up—if I may leave it here, Nan, and pop up when I get the chance?'

'There's another box coming up later,' said Marge eagerly. 'Shall I bring that up, too? You had a field day, I heard, almost emptied the shelves.'

He was like a cat with a saucerful of cream, almost purring, loving teasing them. 'That shop of yours has got to be the best stocked outside of London, Woolworths and Selfridges rolled into one. And don't worry about the other carton, Marge, if you keep it in Reception, I'll collect it some time during the morning.'

'Oh, pity,' said Marge. 'Well, folks, I'll love you and leave you. Things to do and a reception desk to man. It'll be like a battlefield down there today.'

'Our signal to go, too,' murmured Nan, collecting coffee-mugs and plates. Her eyes, full of love, met Callum's. 'You haven't had much to eat,' she added, trying to keep her voice from wobbling, 'and you usually enjoy your food.'

He waved food aside. 'I'm a man in love,' he said huskily. 'Who cares about food?' He held out his arms.

Nan dodged round him and put the dirty dishes in the kitchen. 'Until the next time you're ravenous,' she said wryly.

Callum took her hand. 'Come on, let's go down and do some work. It's the only way I can keep my hands off you.'

Nan went to her office to make phone calls and

Callum to his surgery to open up for a short early session.

'There won't be many in on Christmas Eve,' Myrtle, his receptionist, had assured him. 'Mostly repeat prescriptions.'

He and Nan had arranged to meet to start the round at ten o'clock. She had plenty to do before then.

The first call she made was, as usual, to Truro for news of Hugh. Last night the news had been good. He'd been moved out of Intensive Care onto the orthopaedic ward, where he would receive the specialist attention that he needed.

To her delight, she got through directly to the ward sister, someone with whom she'd had dealings over the years and had met on visits to Truro.

'Gaynor, how lovely to speak to you. I've missed you each time I rang. Now, tell me, horse's-mouth stuff, how is Hugh doing? And, please, don't say as well as can be expected.'

Gaynor laughed. 'You've been talking to my new staff nurse. She's jolly good, but a stickler for obeying the rules. OK, about Hugh. The top of his fibula took a lot of putting together and his tibia was fractured, too, just beneath the head. But it was a clean break and has been pinned and fixated. The patella is the real problem. It took hours to put the pieces together and it's still touch and go whether it will work. He may still end up with an immobile knee and, either way, it's going to be a long job.'

Nan was shattered. She'd hoped for better news, though her observations on the day he'd had his accident had indicated something like this. 'What are the chances of me having a word with him?' she asked.

'Later this morning,' suggested Gaynor, 'if he's up to it. He's still a bit woozy from night sedation at the moment. I'll make sure that the telephone is wheeled into him and he can ring you.'

'Right, tell him I rang, Gaynor, please. It's so frustrating, not being able to get in to see him, but as soon as the thaw sets in I'll be over like a shot.'

Nan said goodbye and put down the phone. For a moment, fleetingly, she was sorry that her Christmas wish for snow had come true. If it hadn't been for the snow, Hugh wouldn't have had his fall and he would be here, doing the round with her, not Callum. But it was only a fleeting thought. Much as she deeply regretted Hugh's accident, she just couldn't help but rejoice that she and Callum had been brought together again.

Their round of the short-term wards didn't take long. Except for a few people, like Glenda Woods, the Raynaud's patient who had only come in the previous day, and three other people whom they were keeping in more for combined social and sickness reasons, they were all fit enough to go home, though there were two patients whom Callum had doubts about.

Frank Moor was one. He had developed bronchitis after a viral infection and was still running a slight temperature. He was a generally rather frail man in his sixties and would be looked after by his wife. Callum had met her when she'd been visiting the day before and had thought that she didn't look too brilliant healthwise, but there was no doubt about how much she wanted him home.

'We'll rub along, Doctor,' she'd told Callum when he'd asked her if she would be able to manage, adding with a surprisingly cheeky sly grin, 'Besides, I wouldn't trust him with a couple of drinks inside him and all these pretty nurses around. I want him home where I can see him.'

Callum had grinned and winked at her and had virtually promised that Frank could go home.

'But only on condition,' he said now to Frank, who was sitting up and already dressed, 'that you come back at once if your temperature goes up or you feel unwell.'

'Don't worry, Doctor. Ella will have me back in at the drop of a hat if my temperature starts to go up again. She was quite scared when it soared to a hundred and three and, to tell the truth, so was I.'

'OK, Frank, in that case, give her a ring and let her have the good news. Finish off your antibiotics and have a great Christmas.' And a really smart doctor would have advised laying off the alcohol, he thought, but, what the hell, this might be their last Christmas together.

Frank shook his hand and thanked him and then offered his hand to Nan and to Joan Weatherall. 'Thanks for everything, Matron, and you, Sister, you have a good Christmas, too. Afraid we won't get to the carol service this year, but I'm sure it'll be a cracker as always.'

The other patient Callum was considering for a short temporary discharge, with the proviso that she return if there were any problems, was Sheila Baker. Sheila was a young married woman with severe lumbago due to a trapped sciatic nerve, causing acute pain. She'd been in for a week on bed rest, conservative physio and regular painkillers delivered through a drip on the press of a button.

The treatment was just beginning to pay off and ideally Callum would have liked to continue with it, uninterrupted, before starting her on a programme of weight-bearing and walking, which was what Hugh Latimer had intended.

Now Callum and Nan and Joyce stood beside her bed, a trio of professionals knowing that they should resist the pleading in Sheila's eyes as she begged to be allowed to go home for Christmas.

'I must be there for the twins, particularly. They're nearly three, just at an age to appreciate the tree and the presents. And Roy's been so wonderful over all this.' She waved her hand over her leg, protected by a cradle. 'I want to be there with him. He was away last Christmas...' Her eyes filled with tears and she laid a hand on Callum's arm. 'Please, Dr Mac, let me go home. It doesn't have to be for a week even, just till the day after Boxing Day. I'm sure that Dr Latimer would have let me.'

Callum read the instructions in Hugh's neat handwriting about continuous treatment and was by no means sure that he would have. For the first time since he'd arrived at the hospital he found himself in a medical dilemma. This patient was Hugh's patient, not his, and when he'd written the note about continuous treatment he would have known that Christmas had been looming.

He moved a foot or two away from the bed and stared out of the window. Make a clinical judgement, he told himself. What would be achieved by pressing Sheila to stay in? Nothing, common sense told him. She would be too distraught to co-operate and her pain would increase. OK, she was going to get a lot of pain anyway if she went home. They could give her an injection before she went. That would hold her for a few hours, but after that she would have to rely on oral painkillers. But if she was in pain but happy...

He became aware that Nan was standing close. He knew it was her because of the delicate scent she used and which clung to her all day.

Without being told, she knew what was troubling him most. She said softly, 'I think there may be a solution to controlling her pain. We've got a couple of TENS packs in the stores, present from The Friends. We've used them with some success when patients begin to get up and about or occasionally for women in labour. They're not supposed to leave the premises but...'

A wide grin split his face. 'I'm not to know that, am I? I'm just an ignorant locum.' With difficulty he stopped himself from giving her a hug and a kiss. 'Go fetch it, Matron, or send one of your minions.'

Joan went herself to collect it from the stores. She put a finger to her lips. 'Least said, soonest mended,' she mouthed. 'No point in involving anyone else. I'll show Sheila how to use it and swear her to secrecy.' She was obviously enjoying the little drama.

Callum thought for the umpteenth time that Tintore Cottage Hospital was just about the best place to be to enjoy an old-fashioned Christmas. It was awash with goodwill—the genuine article, not dependent on money and expensive gifts.

He gave Sheila the good news that she could go home for a couple of days, then he and Nan continued the round in the long-stay unit. There wasn't anything here for Callum to decide. It had been known for days, and in some cases weeks, who would be going to relatives for the holiday.

Sam Woods, ninety-something, mildly diabetic, went every year to his granddaughter and her family. Reg Arbuthnot, in his eighties, an ex-sergeant major who'd lost his leg in the Second World War and was also partially blind, was going to stay with his sister for a few days.

'If they last the course,' murmured Nan to Callum. 'He's often back by lunchtime on Boxing Day.'

'Why on earth does he go?' asked Callum.

'Tradition,' said Nan. 'They promised their mum that they would always spend Christmas together while they were both alive.'

Callum was astounded. 'Do you mean that old Sergeant Major Arbuthnot, that great big giant of a man who scares me to death even though he's half-blind and only has one leg, still sticks to a promise he must have made decades ago?'

Nan nodded. 'That's right. He's a great stickler for tradition. Goes to what he calls Church Parade every Sunday, belongs to the British Legion, though there aren't many left of his generation. Some of his cronies come up occasionally to play cards. They're quite a bunch of characters.'

They were in the corridor between the upstairs sitting room and the long-stay bedrooms. There was no one about. Callum lifted Nan off her feet and swung her round.

'My dearest...' he kissed her '...darling...' he kissed her again '...girl.' Kisses were scattered over her face and hair and neck. 'The whole place is thick with characters. I've met a few in my time, scattered all over the world, but never so many in one place.' He put her down carefully as if she were cut glass. 'Nan,' he said softly, 'what is it about this place that seems to breed...?' He paused and added almost shyly, 'Goodness is perhaps the best way to describe it.'

He was being serious and she answered him thoughtfully. 'I don't rightly know, Callum. I've wondered about it sometimes. Perhaps it's because the Hopkinsons who owned the fish factories and many of the fishing boats were good employers. Even when the factories closed down there was a fund in trust to compensate the people who lost their jobs. In a small community they made a huge impact. Oh, we've got a few bad apples, but they're kept in order by the rest of the community.'

One of the bedroom doors down the corridor opened and an elegant elderly lady emerged and began walking toward them, leaning heavily on a frame.

'Doctor, just the gentleman I wanted to see...' She speeded up.

Nan muttered under her breath, 'It's Miss Lilian Bancroft. You missed her yesterday—she was out visiting. She's a right old gossip. Tell her you'll talk to her later.' She looked at her watch. 'We must get up to Tiddlywinks and sort out the kids for discharge.'

She sped off in the direction of the children's ward, leaving Callum to extricate himself from Lilian's busy tongue.

He joined her remarkably quickly. 'What did you do to Lilian?' she asked in surprise. 'Lay her out cold?'

Callum grinned and laid a forefinger against his nose. His eyes twinkled. 'That's for me to know and you to guess,' he said.

The children were quickly sorted. The asthmatic

Thompson twins could go home, and so could Peter, clumsy as he was with his plaster cast.

'But not till later this afternoon,' Nan reminded Callum, when he told them they could go any time. 'They're all in the nativity play.'

Callum gave a deep-throated chuckle and smote his forehead theatrically. 'Of course. Whatever was I thinking about? The show must go on.'

Polly and the children looked at him as if he were mad, but saw that it was meant to be funny and rolled about laughing.

The phone rang and Nan, who was nearest the office, answered it.

Marge said, 'I've got Molly Short on the line. She sounds just a wee bit excited. I think your other wish may be coming true, Nan, and it's on the cards that we'll have a Christmas Eve or Christmas Day baby.'

CHAPTER NINE

NAN pushed close the office door to shut out the babble of children's voices and took a deep, deep breath. 'Put Molly through, Marge.' Her voice wobbled with anticipation. If Molly did give birth on either day, it would be a first for the hospital in her ten years as Matron—and, to crown it all, the new mum would be one of her own nurses. And as if that were not enough, there was Callum—her old love, her only love, whom she'd met over young Lucy when she'd been in labour. It seemed very fitting that they should work together over Molly.

One way and another, this Christmas would be one to remember. She grinned and hugged the receiver to her bosom.

Excitement boiled up in her and she made a valiant effort to squash it. No way must she let Molly sense how excited she was. She needed to be calm for her. It might be a false alarm, she wasn't due for three weeks...

'You're through to Matron, Molly,' she heard Marge say.

'Matron.' Molly's voice was trembling, breathless. 'I think I've started. All night I've been having little twitches and twinges. I don't know if they're proper contractions. They're not regular or strong, but... Oh, I'm not being very coherent, am I?'

Nan chuckled. 'No, you're not, love, are you? Never mind. Now, let's get the obvious out of the way first. Could these possibly be Braxton-Hicks' contractions?'

'I'm pretty sure they're not. I had some a week or two ago—actually, while Dr Latimer was examining me—and he confirmed that's what they were. These aren't like that. They're not as definite and yet they seem more like the real thing somehow.'

'And you haven't had a show of blood or mucus or any sort of discharge?'

'Nothing... It's just that...I have this feeling. I just think that I'm going to burst.'

Nan smiled to herself. She had that feeling, too. She said softly, 'I think, Molly, that you'd better pack your little overnight bag and let us have a look at you. If it's a false alarm then you can make yourself useful, helping out over the holiday. Does that appeal to you? And if it's not, then the sooner we have you comfortably installed in the maternity suite, the better.'

There was a huge sigh of relief from the other end of the phone. 'Oh, Matron, I was hoping you'd say that. Doreen—you know, my sister-in-law—wants me to stay with her, but I'd much rather be at the hospital with you and my own crowd. What time shall I come?'

'What about any time now so that we can get you sorted before lunch?'

'Yes, please. Doreen will bring me up. Thank you, Matron, you're brilliant.'

And soft in the head, thought Nan as she put the receiver down. You need your brain tested, Winters. As if there isn't enough to do, without wishing for a Christmas baby with all that entails. You or Joyce will be on duty or on call tonight and perhaps tomorrow night—and, of course, Callum, too, for the epidural.

It was a solemn thought, but it didn't stop her bubbling over with anticipation when she relayed the news to Callum moments later. He was hovering outside the office door, as if he'd realised that it was an important call.

'You're mad, woman,' he whispered, squeezing her round her waist. His laughing eyes gleamed. A hank of hair which had started off being brushed back, making him look distinguished, fell across his forehead, making him look, instead, rather rakish. He pushed it back with a gesture that she remembered from times past. 'But I must admit it would be fun, a Christmas Eve baby born at midnight. It would be a first for me. Let's put in an order right now.' He looked up at the angel on top of the tree. 'If you've got any pull with *you know who*, we want to order one baby, please, on the stroke of midnight tonight, sex not important.'

Nan giggled. 'You're more of a romantic idiot than I am,' she murmured. 'I don't think that I should let you loose on my patients.'

'It's that Celtic blood in me, all mystical and otherworldly, that will out in spite of my scientific training.' His hand was still round her waist, making her skin tingle. 'Do you know that legend has it that all the beasts in the fields kneel down at midnight on Christmas Eve?'

Nan shook her head, her green eyes misty. 'I hadn't heard that one,' she said. 'I like it, it's a beautiful thought.'

'I've another beautiful thought.' Callum murmured. 'Picturing you, holding a newborn baby to your breast, with your shining hair rippling down your back, a perfect madonna and child.'

Nan felt goose pimples creep up her arms and across the back of her neck. His voice was low and throaty, his burr pronounced and throbbing with love. Did he really see her like that, a pure symbol of mother love?

She was startled when Polly gave a polite little cough—she had forgotten where she was. She and Callum had seemed to be alone, the ward and the children having faded away. 'Excuse me, Matron, Doctor, have you finished your round? We really need to do one more rehearsal before this afternoon and I'd like to do it before the children's dinners come up.' Polly's pretty little face looked stern and determined. This was her first Christmas production and it was going to be the best.

Casually Callum slipped his arm from round Nan's waist and, looking contrite, replied with a smile to melt an iceberg, 'Polly, *I'll* be out of your hair in no time. I'll just check Bobby Lawson's arm, though, according to the night report, he slept well and is obviously in good form this morning. He's certainly not going to need specialling tonight.' He glanced at Nan, one eyebrow quirked quizzically, just as if he hadn't been making love to her with his voice and eyes moments before. 'But I don't know what Matron's plans are.'

The nerve of the man, Nan thought, almost suggesting that she had nothing else to do but clutter up Tiddlywinks for the rest of the morning. She struggled to hold back a blush that suddenly threatened. 'If you don't need me, Doctor,' she said quickly, formally, blinking to break eye contact, 'I'll go and get on with organising the room for the new admission to Maternity.'

It was a good diversion, as she'd known it would be. Polly's eyes grew round with curiosity, pleading to know the details but too polite to ask.

Nan took pity on her. 'It's Molly Short,' she explained, 'She's coming in, a precautionary move more than anything, but, well, with her husband away...'

Polly reacted exactly on cue. Her pretty young face lit up. 'Oh, wouldn't it be super, Matron, if she had a Christmas baby?'

'Super,' agreed Nan as she made for the door, away from Callum's hungry eyes.

The maternity suite, tucked away in its own little corridor behind the nurses' station, was buzzing as it hadn't done for weeks. The last baby to be delivered there had been at the beginning of December.

Carrie Davis, the short-stay ward auxiliary who was seconded to Maternity when it was occupied and who checked it every day, keeping it in a state of readiness, was busy wiping down the already gleaming surfaces in the milk kitchen, conscious of the fact that Matron and Sister Joyce, the assistant matron, were next door, getting the room ready for Molly's admission.

She could hear bits and pieces of their conversation—mostly technical stuff about timing between contractions and during contractions and about dilatation of the cervix and rupturing of the membranes, which she thought of as the waters breaking. And they were wondering at what point Dr Mac would decide to give Molly her epidural—they seemed to think that it would be sooner rather than later in her labour.

That was a new one. Usually they had to get a

doctor out from Truro to do epidurals, but, apparently, this lovely hunk of a man who'd dropped in out of the blue a couple of days ago was qualified to do it. Matron was said to be over the moon that they wouldn't have to ask Truro to send someone.

A familiar wave of excitement washed over her. She might be only on the fringes of the birth of the babies born in the unit, keeping everything ultra-clean and being at everyone's beck and call, but she was intensely proud of being treated as one of the team. She certainly wouldn't mind working all day and all night if it meant that she could be around for this baby—a Christmas baby, born to one of their own.

There was a knock at the outer door of the unit.

'See who it is, please, Carrie,' Matron called.

Carrie opened the door to find Dr Mac standing outside, leaning against the doorjamb. He looked gorgeous, with his hair rather ruffled and that certain smile on his face that somehow made you feel special. I wonder if he and Matron... After all, they were old friends...

Putting his finger to his lips, he said in a loud theatrical whisper, 'Carrie, do you think that Matron would let a mere man enter these hallowed portals, this females-only zone?'

Before Carrie could answer, Matron called out, 'Carrie, tell Dr Mac to stop playing the fool and come in.'

There was no way Carrie was going to tell this big charming man to stop playing the fool. She opened the door wide and, smiling, almost bobbed a curtsy. 'Come in, Doctor,' she said softly, lapsing as even some of the young people did into local idiom. 'You'm very welcome.'

'Thanks, Carrie, you're a peach,' he replied, stepping into the short corridor.

He strode into the room which Nan and Joyce were preparing for Molly. 'Glad to find you both here,' he said. 'I'd like a word about this epidural...' The rest of his words were lost to Carrie as he quietly closed the door behind him.

A little while later, when Carrie was cleaning the bath and shower room, the three of them left—the doctor and Sister Joyce a little ahead of Matron, who poked her head round the bathroom door, before following the other two.

'Everywhere looks smashing, Carrie, as always, thanks to you. Molly will be here before lunch so, please, let the kitchen know that you may want another meal sent up, though whether Molly will want to eat is anybody's guess—depends on how things are. Sister Joyce or I will be up to examine her when she arrives so we'll know more then.'

Carrie clapped her hands together almost as if she were praying, her blue eyes sparkling. 'Oh, Matron, wouldn't it be fabulous if she does have her baby tonight? Tintore's first Christmas Eve baby.'

Nan laughed and imitated Carrie's gesture. 'Dr Mac has already put in an order for one baby to be delivered at midnight, and he usually gets what he wants,' she said. 'And everyone seems to be rooting for it so if prayers and wishes are to be answered it's just got to happen.'

Carrie shrugged. 'Oh, well,' she said, 'if Dr Mac's put in an order, I guess that's that. Who would dare say no to him?' She met Nan's eyes and they both burst into laughter.

'Who, indeed,' Nan replied, thinking that her prediction that Callum would sweep in and break all the female hearts in the vicinity had indeed happened.

Winters, you can't get much more unprofessional than that, she scolded herself as she made her way briskly to her office. The grapevine will be humming with the news that Matron and Dr Mac have confirmed that Molly's baby will be born tonight.

Forty minutes later, Nan straightened up, ducked out from under the sheet draped over Molly's drawn-up knees and beamed at her.

'You were quite right, Molly. The contractions are for real, the genuine article. Your cervix is beginning to dilate and I'd say that everything is on course for a straightforward delivery. Now, I'm going to listen to the baby's heartbeat again and check the strength and timing of the contractions.'

Molly said, 'There's one coming now.' She rolled over on her side, pulled her knees up as far as she could and grunted. 'That was much stronger than any of the others,' she panted as the contraction began to subside.

Nan was checking her fob watch. 'And a pretty long one,' she said. 'Now, choice time. Nothing's going to happen for a good while yet—your membrane is still intact. Do you want to get up, sit in the chair, wander around in here or out as far as the nurse's station? If you're hungry, you can have a very light lunch if you want it—a yoghurt or something. Some mums find it gives them energy and staying power, but it's entirely up to you at this stage.'

Molly gave a hiccuping laugh. 'And at what stage do I cease to have a choice, Matron?'

Nan laughed, too. 'Oh, in a few hours' time, when

you want to do all sorts of weird and wonderful things and Sister Joyce and I have to persuade you that cleaning the windows in a snowstorm really isn't a good idea.'

Molly said shyly, 'Oh, I've done all the nesting bits. I was up most of last night, tidying the airing cupboard, doing a bit of ironing. That's when I felt sure that the funny twinges I was getting were contractions and the baby was imminent. When I had the Braxton-Hicks' it wasn't like that.' She swivelled round to sit on the side of the bed and looked directly at Nan. 'But just how imminent is it, Matron?'

Patting Molly's arm, Nan said, 'You know that I can't tell you that, Molly. Labour takes its own time and differs for everybody, and that's especially true of a first baby—'

She broke off as Molly started to breathe heavily and clasp her hands round her 'bump'. She examined her watch again as the rhythmic pain built up to a crescendo and then began to fade again, leaving Molly red-faced and panting.

'See what I mean?' Nan said softly. 'You haven't settled into a pattern yet. There may be some more biggies on the way or much weaker ones but, whatever, I think perhaps going for a walk outside the unit isn't now an option.' She stood up. 'I'm going to send Carrie in to keep you company, but would you like me to phone Doreen and ask her to come back and sit with you this afternoon? You need someone around, though Sister or I don't need to be with you all the time at this stage.'

Molly shook her head. 'Not Doreen. She means well, but she'll terrify me, going on about the bad time she had with her four.' Suddenly her face crumpled and a few tears trickled down her cheeks. 'I do wish my Russell was here. He'd know what to do. He went to all the classes with me and now he won't even be here when the baby's born.'

Nan wrapped her arms round Molly's bulky body. 'Is there someone else I can get hold of to be with you at the birth? You've got loads of friends.'

'Nearly all my friends are here at the hospital, and either on duty or getting ready for Christmas in their precious time off. It wouldn't be fair.'

'I don't think any of them would see it like that,' murmured Nan. 'I think they'd be proud to do it. Who would you most like to have around, help you pant and rub your back?'

'Ella,' Molly said without hesitation. 'We've known each other since forever, but she's helping to special old Dr Horton, so that's no good.'

'Dr Mac decided on the round this morning that Dr Horton doesn't need specialling any more. Against all the odds he's improving by leaps and bounds, so Ella is almost surplus to requirements. I'll ask her to come and see you—I dare say she'll hotfoot it here anyway once she hears that you've arrived. If she's willing, and I'm sure that she will be, she can have the afternoon off while Carrie's with you and come back during the evening. How does that sound?'

'Too good to be true,' said Molly tremulously. 'It would be great if she could be with me, almost like family. As you know, I'm short of family on my side.'

Nan knew. Molly's parents and her two siblings had been killed in a motor accident a few years before.

She got up and crossed to the door. 'Well, we're all your family, my love, and there will be a bunch of us with you all the time. Now, I'll go and organise that sitting roster. You're in for a busy afternoon. Dr Mac will be in to see you to check you over for the epidural and fill you in on exactly what he's going to do.'

'Matron,' Molly called, as Nan reached the door, 'I'm sorry I won't be able to go to the Tiddlywinks nativity play, but I hope that you and Dr Mac will be able to go...' She hesitated and blushed. 'Is he as nice as everyone says he is?'

For some obscure reason, Nan found herself blushing, too. 'He's a man in a million,' she heard herself say, 'and a wizard of a doctor. He'll take good care of you, Molly.'

'You're late,' Nan muttered at Callum a couple of hours later as he slid into the other VIP seat beside her in the front row of the 'stalls'. 'We're just about to begin.'

'Been checking Molly out,' he murmured. 'Don't foresee any difficulties with the epidural. She's a sensible woman, as one would expect of one of your nurses, and will co-operate, no problem.'

He looked about him. Tiddlywinks had been transformed. He smiled at the transformation. There was yet more tinsel, more balloons and coloured streamers. Polly, with help from some of the mums, had rigged up as a stage a pair of heavy velvet curtains, liberally decorated with silver stars, which didn't quite meet in the middle but satisfactorily divided the players from the audience.

One of the mums was sitting at the side of the curtains, strumming softly on a guitar a medley of carols and Christmas songs.

'Wayne's mum, Annette,' Nan reminded Callum, 'who played so beautifully the day before yesterday.'

He nodded. 'I remember.' He turned to look at Nan and found her face turned toward him. He leaned forward and mouthed, '*I love you with all my heart*,' just as if they were alone and not in a room full of people. His hazel eyes, a blend of green and gold with occasional flecks of brown, shone brilliantly, luminous with warmth and passion. The chairs were close together and Nan could see every one of his long, dark blond lashes tipped with gold.

For a moment her heart seemed to stand still, then it began to beat a wild tattoo that sent her robin redbreast bosom rising and falling. She could almost feeling him reaching out for her—*almost* feel his arms round her. She was finding it difficult to breathe. All she could do was gaze helplessly into his eyes that said so much more than words could.

'You're crackers,' she mouthed back, trying to make light of the intense moment.

Annette strummed several loud chords on her guitar, the curtains, pulled by a pair of other mums, rattled shakily back and scene one was revealed.

Like a puppet on a string, Nan's head was jerked round and she found herself staring at scene one. Calling on all her years of experience, and making a tremendous effort, she steamrollered over her treacherous, wandering thoughts, crashed down to earth and concentrated hard on the play.

It was the least she could do. Polly and the mums and kids had worked like Trojans to put on their show. Beside her she felt Callum rearranging himself in his chair and leaning forward as he, too, came down from cloud nine, or whatever level he'd been on.

Nan registered a splodgy backdrop of distant mountains thickly plastered with snow, which appeared every year, and a signpost announcing in gold lettering, THIS WAY TO BETHLEHEM.

To the left of centre stage Peter clumped along, with his plastered foot dragging, wearing an overlarge, old-fashioned camelhair dressing-gown that reached the floor—probably purloined by Polly from one of the oldies, thought Nan. On his head he wore a striped teatowel secured with a circlet of tinsel, and on his chin a cotton-wool beard haphazardly dyed brown.

On the battered sledge he was jerkily pulling behind him, Wendy, their pretty little diabetic, her gold curly hair half-covered by a dark blue silk scarf, was clinging on like grim death to the sides of the sledge.

There was silence for a moment, and then her breathless voice piped out. 'Peter... No, I mean, Joseph, are we nearly there? Have we reached Bethlehem? I'm getting so tired, I think the baby's going to come soon.'

Peter-Joseph stopped suddenly and Wendy nearly catapulted off the sledge. He pointed to the signpost. 'Not far to go now, Mary,' he said. 'We'll soon have you tucked up in bed in hospital and Dr Mac and Matron will come and help you have the baby Jesus.'

Callum's shoulders shook and a ripple of amusement ran round the circle of seats.

Peter glared at the audience and said firmly, 'We don't know yet that there's not going to be room at the hospital, or at the inn, and that Jesus is going to be born in a stable.'

This time, though there were still a lot of smiling faces, a murmur of sympathy and support and a ripple of applause ran through the audience.

Wendy also rallied to the defence of her co-star. 'Well, of course Joseph wanted me to the hospital where Matron and Dr Mac could look after me, but I think it will be nice to have my baby in a stable,' she shrilled indignantly. 'It's nice and warm there, with the animals breathing all over everything.'

Everybody applauded and Tom Barnard, standing at the back of the ward, called out, 'You tell 'em, love.'

Peter-Joseph said, 'Well, we've got to get on and get to Bethlehem before dark.' He started to pull the sledge to the opposite side of the stage. 'The next scene,' he announced, before disappearing offstage, 'is in the stable in Bethlehem and there will be music and angels and things, because the baby Jesus will have been born.'

The curtains were rattled together and Annette played loudly on her guitar in an attempt to drown out the sound of movement from behind the curtains. There was a lot of scuffling—a bark—a bleat?

The audience were still applauding Joseph and Mary, and Callum said softly, leaning toward Nan, 'What an exit line. Eat your hearts out, all you professionals—you're not a patch on these kids. How do you do it, Nan? How do you get everyone to pull together and bring out that certain something in them?'

'I'm not guilty,' Nan replied, avoiding his dancing eyes. 'This was all Polly's doing.'

The second scene, which took a long time to set up, brought tears to a lot of eyes and a round of applause when the curtains went up. Even Callum's eyes glittered suspiciously.

All the children, except Bobby Lawson, were on stage, plus a few siblings to make up the numbers.

Harry, their little leukaemia boy, his downy, newly growing fuzz of hair gleaming redly in the bright lights Polly had rigged up with help from Dave, was near the front of the stage. He was wearing a striped, man-sized pyjama jacket that reached to his knees, and his feet were bare. In one hand he was carrying a cage containing two chirpy budgies, while his other hand was firmly clutching the collar of a large sheep.

'A shepherd?' hazarded Callum.

'Representing all three shepherds, I should think, just as we have two kings and not three. In spite of the extras Polly seems to have drafted in, there are barely enough for the major parts—quite apart from the Angel Gabriel and the host of angels.'

She grinned at Callum's puzzled expression. 'I'm lost,' he said.

'Patience.' She chuckled. 'All will be revealed.'

Marie was there, bed and all. She was dressed in a white theatre gown, draped about with silver tinsel, and she carried a wand with a star on top, which she waved around imperiously.

'Angel or fairy?' asked Callum, low-voiced.

Nan shook her head. 'No idea. Does it matter?'

'Not at all,' murmured Callum, sliding his hand over hers. 'She looks delightful.' This time Nan didn't try to avoid his eyes or pull her hand from his. She didn't want to. There was a magic about everything this afternoon, she mused dreamily, first Molly, now this lovely, touching, sincere, children's version of the old story. It was, of course, the sincerity that made it.

She and Callum looked at each other for a moment, silly, loving smiles on their faces, then turned back to the stage.

It was the traditional stable scene if one accepted— in place of oxen, donkeys and sheep—a couple of dogs, an angora rabbit, several cats, a budgie, some white mice, a hibernating tortoise that could just be seen and one token, authentic, biblical-looking sheep.

Held in their nervous owners' arms or on leads, they were all doing their own thing, barking, mewing and baaing. They were grouped round Joseph and Mary and the baby Jesus. He was vigorously kicking his legs and lying in a carrycot heavily disguised as a manger, with straw hanging over the sides.

'Wendy's brother,' Nan whispered to Callum, 'born in September.'

'My word, both starring roles in one family,' said Callum. 'Bet their mum's proud of them.'

'Envy of the other mums, I guess,'

Suddenly, Polly's voice rang out clearly over some sort of loudspeaker system that Dave must have rigged up, 'And the Angel of The Lord was with them and a host of angels and glory shone around.'

There was a murmur of voices and a lot of scuffling at the back of the stage. Then Bobby Lawson, his arm in a sling and a pair of outsize wings attached to a white nightdress worn backwards, suddenly appeared standing on some sort of platform so that he towered above the manger.

'You've forgotten your halo' came a loud whisper, and a pair of hands passed him up a gold spiky circlet, rather like the one on the Statue of Liberty.

It took him a moment to fix it on his head by a wire frame and, red-faced, in his gruff voice he chanted, 'Fear not, I am the Angel Gabriel come down from heaven to be with the baby Jesus and with you all on this special day, His birthday.'

He stretched out his good arm in a sort of blessing, Annette began to play, softly at first and then louder, and from both sides of the stage a number of children, dressed as angels, filed onto the stage, singing joyfully at the tops of their voices, 'Happy Birthday to You, Happy Birthday to You, Happy Birthday dear Jesus, Happy Birthday to You.'

CHAPTER TEN

THE applause was thunderous and everyone joined in as Happy Birthday was repeated several times. Then the curtains were finally drawn together and the children, carrying or leading the animals for which they were responsible, streamed off stage and rushed to join proud parents. Dave, who must have been helping out during the performance, appeared, pushing a flushed, happy little Marie in her bed.

Callum looked a bit anxious. 'Hope that little one hasn't overdone it,' he murmured to Nan.

Nan smiled up at him, her heart in her eyes, loving him for caring so much. 'Stop being a doctor for a moment,' she said. 'Look at her—does she look as if she's in pain? Her mother and Polly would have kept an eye on her. Now I'm going to congratulate Polly and the mums and see if they need any help clearing up.'

Polly went pink with embarrassment and happiness when Nan told her that it had been the best Christmas play ever. But she refused help with clearing up and shooed them out through the curtains, pointing out that that was where their duty lay. It was Polly at her bossiest.

'Well, we seem to have been given our marching orders…' Nan laughed '…so let's go join in the junketings.'

The party was as traditional as the play itself. The children had small gifts, forerunners of the presents that they would receive on Christmas Day and there were crackers to pull and silly hats and party games.

They stayed just long enough to pull a few crackers and say goodbye to the children who were being discharged home for Christmas, before making their way to Maternity to check on Molly.

'What a play—what a party,' said Callum, as he strode along beside Nan, his swinging hand occasionally brushing against hers. 'Whoever thought of singing "Happy Birthday, dear Jesus", instead of something more traditional, was a genius. There wasn't a dry eye in the house by the time we'd finished.'

He swung his arms even more vigorously. 'Altogether, it's been a great day. The old doctor so much improved against all the odds and the kids, even little Marie and our little leukaemia chap in great form... and you and me, love, working side by side. What more could one ask? It's magic.'

He slanted a smile down at Nan, but didn't slow up.

Almost running to keep up with him, Nan thought. He's on a real high.

'Magic time of year,' she panted. 'Are you sure you didn't lace the kids' lemonade you were swigging with a spot of gin or vodka?'

He caught her hand for a moment and brought it to his lips. 'Don't need alcohol or any other stimulant when you're around,' he murmured.

They were almost at the nurses' station. A couple of nurses were there, heads bent over charts.

Nan tugged her hand away. 'For heaven's sake, slow down,' she puffed. 'We're not competing in a marathon.'

He stopped abruptly. 'Sorry.' He grinned at her.

'The way I feel now, I could *win* a marathon. I'd go into battle, wearing my lady's favour and nothing would stop me.' His eyes seemed to devour her.

Nan felt herself glowing all over and shivering. She didn't feel thirty-five, or even twenty-five, but more like fifteen and out on a first date.

'Idiot,' she whispered when she got her breath back. She had to bring him down to earth. In this elated mood heaven only knew what he might say next, and in front of whom? He was doing it again, making love to her with his eyes and silly words.

'Aren't you mixing your metaphors, knights and winning marathons?' she asked, trying to sound matter-of-fact. She searched for something innocuous to say before he came up with some nonsense reply. 'By the way, those crackers that you provided for the kids must have cost the earth. They had such brilliant presents in them—dolls, cars, planes, real quality stuff. I didn't know that the shop stocked anything quite so exotic and pricey.'

He looked smug. 'They were good weren't they? Old stock, according to the lady behind the counter. They came up with some lovely surprises.'

He was looking so complacent, as if he was hugging a secret to himself, that Nan would have liked to have asked what specifically, but sensibly held her tongue. She inspected her fob watch. 'Let's get on. I've masses to do after we've checked on Molly.'

Molly was greedily gulping in gas and air when they arrived and rather reluctantly put aside the mask in order that they might examine her. Her contractions were settling into a regular pattern and getting stronger, but the membrane was still intact and she was dilating only slowly. It looked as if it was going to be a long, slow labour.

That wasn't unusual for a first birth but, with everyone rooting for a Christmas Eve Baby, they were all conscious of time plodding inexorably on.

Nan handed Molly back the mask as soon as she and Callum had finished the examination, and Molly eagerly took some deep gulps. But she managed a shaky, almost teasing smile and asked. 'Do you think that I might still have a midnight baby, Dr Mac, just as you ordered?'

So that had got about, thought Callum, glancing at Nan and catching her eye. Someone had spilled the beans. He watched fascinated as she flushed a delicate guilty rose. He grinned. Lovely to see a woman who could still blush and do it so beautifully—funny, he couldn't have made her blush like that ten years ago. She had been a tough cookie then independent, capable, confidently carving out a career for herself.

Callum smiled at Molly. 'Well, it's still on the cards, love, but your baby won't be rushed. It doesn't care a hoot that it's Christmas Eve. It'll come in its own time when it's good and ready. Sometimes we have to intervene, but we only do that reluctantly and if really necessary, and at this moment your baby is doing exactly what it should be doing—getting itself organised for its journey into the big wide world.'

He touched Molly's shoulder gently. 'But it's make your mind up time, love, if you do want this epidural, I must break your waters and get on with it right now, before things go any further.'

Molly screwed up her face as another contraction took hold. When it had subsided, she said breathlessly. 'I'll go for it Doctor, I don't think that I can take much more of this.'

'Wise choice, my dear, we don't want you or the baby getting exhausted. Right, Matron, if you'll assist, we can get started, I'll just go and get scrubbed.'

It didn't take a moment to rupture the membranes and release the fluid, then Nan asked Carrie to fetch the covered trolley already laid up with the instruments that were needed for the epidural. She went through the procedure with Molly as she stood at one side of the bed and rolled Molly over to face her, knees tucked up to round her back as much as possible.

'The most important thing is not to move,' Nan impressed on Mollie, 'just grit your teeth at each contraction.'

Callum returned and picked up the syringe. 'Ready?' he asked Molly, giving her one of his reassuring smiles.

'As I'll ever be,' she panted, with an attempt at a smile.

Callum inserted the large bore epidural needle through the intervertebral space in the lumbar region of the spinal column, and slowly ran through the epidural fluid to dull the pain. The whole procedure took about half an hour.

Carrie, clearly in her element, stood at the head of the bed and stroked Molly's damp hair back from her forehead.

When Callum had finished, Nan phoned Joyce and asked her to come up and take over Molly's supervision. It was hospital policy to have a trained midwife in attendance after a patient had been given an epidural.

Nan helped Molly to roll onto her back. 'The epidural will begin to work soon,' she assured her, 'then you may need help to be aware that contractions are taking place, that's why Sister Joyce will be here with you until I relieve her later.' She smiled across at Carrie. 'And I'm pretty sure that Carrie will be here for the night.'

'You betcha,' said Carrie squeezing Molly's hand.

'Thanks,' puffed Molly and groaned, 'back's killing me.'

'Do you want me to rub it?' asked Carrie.

'Please.' She leaned forward so that Carrie could get to her back and glanced obliquely up at Callum with another smile of sorts. 'But it could still happen, couldn't it?' she mumbled, 'He or she could pop out at the witching hour of midnight.'

'Like Doctor Mac says, he or she just could,' said Nan, deciding that Callum should be let off the hook, he'd been incredibly patient. She moved toward the door. 'Here's Sister Joyce, so we'll be off, but we're all at the ready, love. When the big moment comes we'll all be here.'

In the short corridor leading from maternity to the nurses' station, Callum slid a strong, muscular arm round Nan's waist and whirled her round to face him, planting a long, hard kiss on her mouth that left her breathless and her knees wobbly.

'This grabbing kisses whenever you can,' she murmured breathlessly as he lifted his head, 'is beginning to be a habit.'

'Good habit,' he replied, his voice not too steady. 'Oh, Nan, dear heart, I do love you. I'm grateful for every hour I've got to make up to you for my behaviour all those years ago. I just can't believe that I behaved so badly.'

Nan shook her head. 'Well, neither of us came out smelling of roses. We were both selfish. I didn't really want to go to America, I tried to see it as a career opportunity, but wasn't sure that it was—staying put was my best option. When the Aunt Janet business blew up, I was only too ready to come down to Tintore, though I mistakenly thought that it would be a brief visit.'

'But you'd have come whatever when you realised how ill she was.'

'Yes, but I needn't have broken off our engagement the way I did when you refused to come down to Cornwall with me. I could have explained things better and not flown off the handle. I might have suggested that I would follow you over to America at a later date.'

Callum said softly. 'But we didn't have that sort of relationship did we? We were still committed to keeping everything light even after I told you that I loved you and we got…engaged, nothing had really changed.'

'That's because it was an engagement of convenience, not love, to help you get the job,' Nan stroked her fingers down his cheek, 'though I wanted to believe that you did love me a little, almost did for a short while, especially when Aunt Janet came up to London to meet you. She made it seem real and in a strange way, the fact that she didn't approve of you, made it seem even more valid.'

To her surprise, Callum's cheeks reddened. 'I've a confession to make. The hospital that I was going to, hadn't said anything about having a partner. That was a bit of creative thinking on my part. I suddenly realised that I couldn't bear the thought of going to the states without you. It dawned on me that I had been in love with you from the moment you emerged, neat little bottom first, from doing an internal on that poor kid who was all alone...'

'Lucy,' breathed Nan.

He nodded. 'Lucy. I just wouldn't admit it, not to you, not to myself—it just didn't match my image of the dedicated, single minded career man—the man you knew me as. I knew that you would fall about laughing.'

His eyes were a mist of green and gold.

Nan made a little hissing noise between her teeth and eased herself out of his arms. She took a step backwards. 'Oh, Callum my dear, why didn't you say? All these lost years...'

'You know that it wouldn't have worked had I come clean then, Nan, we were two different people.' He placed his large hands on her shoulders and gave her a beautiful smile. 'Let's not waste any more time on recriminations, let's just bang the drums and sound the trumpets and rejoice that we're together again.'

He kissed her forehead and dropped his hands.

'Well, much as I hate to leave you my darling, I'd best be off,' he said, 'I've a couple of visits to do in the village and a few other chores before showing up for carols.'

Nan reached up and pushed back the hank of hair that had dropped over his forehead. She didn't want to be parted from him even for a short period. She told herself to grow up and be sensible. 'I love you,' she said softly, kissing him on the mouth. 'Carols aren't till seven thirty, come and have a cup of tea with me if you're back before then.'

'Now who's doing the kissing?' he murmured, moving reluctantly away from her.

That had been a couple of busy hours ago, and now they were sitting in her flat, cosy and warm and vibrantly aware of each other, but for some reason unable to break the silence that had manifested itself. The air between them was electric, pulsating. There was so much to say, and yet they both seemed to be dumb. What we really want, thought Nan, is to be in each others' arms making love, there wouldn't be any need for words.

The memory of his muscular arms around her, his sturdy younger body heavy on hers, when they had rushed off from the hospital between spells of duty, to have frantic sessions of frenzied love making, filled her with longing.

She took a gulp of her tea and scrunched on an almond biscuit and prayed for something to say. Out of the blue, she remembered Callum's comment about the singing of Happy Birthday.

'According to Polly, it was the Thompson twins who pointed out with irrefutable logic, that it was HIS birthday,' she announced abruptly.

Callum stopped with a piece of fruit cake half way to his mouth. 'I've lost you,' he said.

'You wanted to know who suggested singing Happy Birthday. It was the Thompson twins. Unconventional, but I must say it was a brilliant idea, I was expecting Away in a Manger or Little Town of Bethlehem or perhaps Twinkle, twinkle little star, great favourites that turn up year after year.'

The penny dropped. Callum's face cleared as he remembered. 'And we got Happy Birthday instead. Bright kids, our two little asthmatics, as are the Lawson twins.' Callum stretched out his long legs and shot Nan a look from hooded eyes. 'I wonder what the odds are on there being two sets of twins in a community of this size—more—or less, than in a larger community?'

'More, I think,' replied Nan, 'if Tintore is anything to go by. We have four sets in the village, not surprising since three pairs are related, so the genes are there and I guess that this probably occurs in close knit communities. Even now that people go further afield to live and work, villagers often marry villagers. The Thompsons are third cousins to the Lawsons for instance.'

'I did wonder, there's a look about them. It's rather like that in the Scottish isles you know. I was a twin, but my sibling, a girl, was stillborn.' He stared into the flickering flames of the almost real gas fire.

Nan sat up with a jerk. This was something else that he had not divulged in the past. All those months together and she had no idea that he was a twin. If, there was any sort of future for them, there was much that they had to learn about each other. He sounded sad and he looked sad, his wide, usually smiling mouth, drooped at the corners.

She said softly, 'You sound as if you still miss her, grieve for her.'

Slowly Callum turned to look at her, his chameleon hazel eyes dark, serious. 'In an odd sort of way, I do, there have been times when I've felt that there was something missing in my life, that it was incomplete.

According to a psychiatrist friend, this is not unknown in twins when one twin doesn't survive.'

He held out his cup for more tea and as Nan poured, he said. 'Would the possibility of twins put you off, Nan?'

Carefully Nan put down the teapot on the low table in front of them and handed him his cup and saucer. Her heart was thundering out erratic beats against her chest wall—surely he must hear them!

She took her time answering, and then, making herself breathe steadily, asked, though she knew the answer. 'Put me off what, Callum?'

'Marrying me...bearing my children. There's a high incidence of twins in my family.'

The firelight flickered on his face—a Greek God sort of face, Nan thought, a solid Greek God rather than a spectacularly handsome one, with his lightly bronzed skin and white blonde hair swept back from his broad forehead. Her heart seemed to have a life of its own, turning over and over in her chest. She had difficulty breathing.

He was asking her to marry him—not lightly, he wasn't hinting. This wasn't about making up for lost time, or spending the rest of his life making love to her, which however truly meant, had a dashing ring to them and the words were perhaps a shade too romantic for their more mature personalities.

Whereas this proposal of marriage was dead serious, frighteningly solemn and her answer must be just as solemn. A binding commitment. It would be the sealing of a bargain, the most serious of bargains. A bargain built round the old fashioned meaning of marriage itself, the procreation of children—her children, Callum's children.

He put down his cup and reached out for her hands which he folded in his. 'Well Nan?' he asked, his soft burr enriching the words, his eyes locked onto hers. 'Would you marry me and take more than a fifty fifty chance of having twins?'

Nan took several deep drawn breaths, just as she often instructed her patients to do to relax them. He didn't say it, but she knew that the doctor in him was thinking—prima gravida at thirty five, and twins! She loved this man, had loved him for a long time, had loved him even when she hadn't realised it the first time around. That's why she had been so angry that he wouldn't support her over Aunt Janet, because in spite of her career to which she had been dedicated, she had loved him with a deep and abiding passion.

She looked down at their entwined hands, hers almost lost in his, then looked back up at him, and said in a gentle husky voice. 'You know, I always rather fancied having...'

The internal phone buzzed. Almost guiltily, as if the caller could see them, they dropped their hands for a moment, but their eyes remained locked onto each other...

Then they exclaimed in unison, 'Molly!'

Joyce confirmed this when Nan picked up the receiver. 'Molly is coming on fast,' said Joyce, 'and I think Callum would like to know.' There was what was sometimes referred to as a significant pause, and then Joyce said with a chuckle. 'I presume that you know the whereabouts of our revered medical officer.'

'I'll pass you over,' said Nan dryly.

He talked to Joyce for a few minutes and then said. 'Right, I'll be down stat.'

He crammed the rest of his cake into his mouth

and took another swig of tea before replacing his cup on the saucer. His eyes looking into Nan's, he murmured. 'Don't forget, we have unfinished business to conclude.' He traced the line of her jaw with one sensitive forefinger.

'I won't forget,' she promised, catching hold of his hand and kissing the palm. 'Tell Joyce that I'll relieve her after the carols have got under way.'

He blew her a kiss from the doorway. 'Will do, love.'

Nan slipped away when they were half through The Holly and the Ivy, and made her way up to maternity. 'Oh the rising of the su-un and the running of the deer...' the assembled voices of the choir and half the villagers followed her up the stairs.

She looked at her watch as she reached the first floor nurses' station—things should be well on the move with Molly.

Molly's room seemed full, but her eyes automatically rested on Callum looming large and reassuring as he bent over Molly.

He straightened up and smiled at Nan. 'Everything's going fine,' he said, 'dilating nicely, no sign of any problems, but we've a way to go yet.'

Molly panted. 'It is going all right isn't it?' She gave Nan a weak smile. 'Thanks for coming, Matron.'

'Wouldn't miss this for anything, love. Now I'm going to stay with you for a while, keep checking the contractions that you can't feel and let Sister Joyce and Doctor Mac go off for a while. I know they'd like to take part in the carol service. Is that okay with you?'

'It's fine,' puffed Molly, as Joyce guided her through the next contraction.

The next few hours were a blur, busy with comings and goings. The epidural safely given, Callum and Joyce went off to put in an appearance at the carol singing, leaving Nan and Ella and Carrie to monitor Molly.

After a while, Nan insisted on Carrie and Ella going for a short break, leaving her alone with Molly.

Molly, beginning to benefit from the epidural and relieved of much of her pain and effort, was almost dozing. For the first time in hours, the room was quiet, yet full of anticipation—biding its time, Nan mused fancifully. In a little while, it would be full of activity again as things built up to a climax.

Palms flat, Nan was feeling Molly's distended abdomen, ready to warn her if a contraction was beginning, that she should push or pant, when Molly opened her eyes.

'He's nice, isn't he,' she said, 'Doctor Mac? Makes you feel safe, and he's got such gentle hands, though they're big.'

Nan felt a huge wave of pride rush through her at this unsolicited praise of Callum. She couldn't believe the depth of love that she had for him. Love that had survived ten years in the desert away from him. Love that had matured as they had both matured. All she wanted now, was to spend the rest of her life with him, where and how didn't matter. Twins or no twins didn't matter.

She felt a faint movement beneath her flat palms spread on Molly's smooth mound of a belly. The movement grew stronger, though because of the epidural Molly was only aware of a 'sensation.'

'Another contraction has started,' warned Nan, 'it's a biggie, but I don't want you to push yet, Molly, you're not fully dilated, just pant and puff, you may feel happier on your side.'

Molly rolled over to face her and puffed and panted. 'Well done,' said Nan, 'if you can roll back, I'll examine you again.' She did a careful vaginal examination. 'You're nearly there love, you're almost fully dilated and the baby will start crowning soon. You must start pushing with the next contraction. This is the really hard part, the baby's in position, the contractions will get stronger as it tries to break through. I want you to take lots of deep breaths between contractions.'

'What—time—is—it?' gasped Molly.

'Nine thirty, the others will be back soon,' said Nan, pushing a damp lock of hair back from Molly's forehead. 'Plenty of time to meet the deadline.'

They were all there as Nan had promised, when the baby, a nine-pound boy, in response to a final, enormous, painful push from Molly, burst out into the world at five minutes to midnight—and yelled loudly at the indignity of it all.

'How's that for delivering on time,' said Callum proudly, smiling down at Molly who was cuddling and crooning over her messy looking baby. 'He's a beautiful little boy, Molly, what are you going to call him?'

Red faced and breathless with effort, but utterly elated, Molly gasped. 'Thomas after my dad...and if you don't mind Doctor Mac, Callum after you... thank you for everything.'

Callum was visibly shaken. 'But my dear,' he said, his voice not quite steady, 'I haven't done anything, you did all the hard work.'

'You were there,' murmured Molly, her eyes on her baby, 'that's what matters. You made me feel so safe.'

EPILOGUE

SEEMING to shiver in the frosty air, the chimes of the church clock struck two as Nan and Callum let themselves into the flat.

There was always plenty to do after a baby was born and they had both been busy, Callum removing the lumbar catheter and completing his examination of Molly and the baby, and Nan and Joyce finishing writing up their joint report.

Then they'd stayed to wet the baby's head with several obligatory cups of tea with Molly and the others. There had been a party atmosphere and everyone had been on a high. They'd been visited by some of the night staff who'd popped in to drool over what they'd considered *their* midnight baby.

Thomas Callum was the common property of Tintore Cottage Hospital.

Callum closed the front door behind them and heaved a huge sigh of relief as he followed Nan into the sitting room. 'Thank God we're alone at last,' he said.

Nan crossed to the drinks cupboard and poured them both a whisky. 'It should be champagne,' she said, clinking her glass to Callum's, 'but I forgot to put it in the fridge before we left. Anyway, here's to Thomas Callum... That's a first in the village, but I bet from now on there'll be quite a few Callums.'

Her Callum smiled into her eyes as their glasses

touched. 'We Celts must stick together,' he murmured, his voice low and rumbly.

They both swallowed a mouthful of whisky, but remained standing about a foot apart in front of the fire—neither seemed to know what to do or say next.

Nan tore her eyes away from his and said in a breathless, wavery sort of voice, 'What a day it's been. I've never known a Christmas Eve like it. So many good things have happened, and to crown it all a Christmas baby.'

She gulped down more whisky and spluttered. They'd said all that before. Why was she so nervous? Why did she have this feeling that something even more momentous was about to happen? Why had she asked Callum back to the flat—it was two o'clock and they should be in bed. They had another busy day ahead of them tomorrow—no, today, Christmas Day, and an early start...

Callum's large, gentle hands were on her shoulders. He bent his head and kissed her nose. 'Nan, stop thinking, planning. Shut down on that conscience of yours. Stop wondering why and listen to your heart and nothing but your heart—that's what I've learned to do over these last few years.'

Nan stared up at him and moistened her lips and wished she could stop being tongue-tied. She wanted to tell him that she loved him, had always loved him, always would, that she wanted his babies, twins or not—but the words just wouldn't come. All those things that she'd been about to tell him when he'd asked her about having twins simply stuck in her throat.

His lovely large warm hands were still on her shoulders, radiating strength and his love for her. She shivered and spilt some whisky down the front of her robin redbreast sweater. She looked down at the damp patch.

'Oh, my lovely cashmere sweater,' she cried. 'I put it on especially for you.' And to her horror, she burst into tears.

Callum took the glass from her fingers and placed it on the table. From somewhere about his person he conjured up a large white handkerchief and mopped up her tears, which were subsiding as quickly as they had begun.

'I'm so sorry,' she muttered. 'How stupid of me.'

'Too much excitement, tears before bedtime,' he murmured, kissing her wet cheeks. 'That's what my mother would say.' He lowered his head and kissed the wet patch on her chest, then sniffed it appreciatively. 'Good Scotch. It blends well with your perfume. As for your sweater, I'll buy you a dozen cashmere sweaters, dear heart, if it will make you happy,' he added, as he folded her into his arms. Still holding her close, he sidestepped toward the sofa.

Nan gave a hiccuping giggle as they sank down into the squashy depths. 'Have you any idea how much cashmere costs?' she asked.

'I've a lot of Christmases and birthdays to make up for,' he replied. 'Oh, Nan, I've dreamed of this moment for years, holding you in my arms again. I dreamed of it, but didn't dare hope that it would ever happen... They were daydreams, but once or twice I had real night dreams about you. Once I even dreamed that you had long hair like this.'

He unpinned her elaborate coil of hair and it tumbled in a rippling, gold-streaked tawny river down to her shoulder blades. 'It's beautiful,' he said, lifting a handful up and sifting the strands through his fingers. 'Shiny and silky and very, very sexy. Who was it said that a woman's hair is her crowning glory?'

'St Paul, I think,' Nan murmured breathily.

'He was dead right,' said Callum. 'If it had been like this in the old days...'

He was right about the sexiness. His fingers in her hair were making all her nerve endings tingle and turning her muscles to jelly. How could he do that to her? They were one-time lovers, for heaven's sake. She knew every inch of his body and he knew every nook and cranny of hers, so why should his hands in her hair make her feel like a quivering, inexperienced teenager?

She shook her head vigorously and the ripples began to tighten up into a cloud of soft curls, as she'd known it would.

For a moment, Callum sat and stared in amazement at the transformation, then put out a tentative hand and stroked the bouncy curls. He rubbed one curl between his thumb and forefinger, stretched it out, then let it spring back.

'My God, woman, have you got any more tricks to drive a man crazy?' he muttered huskily. He pulled her back into his arms and buried his face in her hair. 'If it had been like this ten years ago, I'd never have let you go.'

Her face pressed against his throat, Nan said in a muffled voice, 'I thought you liked it short. Cute but businesslike, you called it.'

'Oh, I did, my love—then.' He lifted his head and cupped her chin so that he could look into her eyes. 'It marked you out for the career-woman that you were, underlined our commitment-free relationship.

We were on equal terms and that's how I wanted it, but now...'

'Now?' Her brilliant green eyes, glowing like emeralds, were only inches from his own.

Callum's chest expanded as he drew in an enormous breath. 'Nan, my dearest love, I want a woman to love and cherish and make my partner for life and be the mother of my children. Can you see yourself in that role, my darling? I'm not asking you to give up all this.' He waved an arm to indicate the whole hospital. 'You've created something too special for that, but I'd like to share it with you, until—'

'All those little twins come along?'

'Are you laughing at me, Miss Winters?' he asked.

Nan shook her head and dimpled, and her curls bounced. 'No, my darling, I'm not laughing at you. Your future is my future and all I ask is that we share it. In fact, I consider us now to be formally engaged.' She kissed him on the mouth. It was a long, firm kiss full of the promise and commitment for which he yearned.

When they came up for air, Callum was breathing heavily. 'Talking of engagements,' he said, heaving himself up so that he could reach into the pocket of his trousers. 'I've something for you, a little present.' He pulled out a small package wrapped in gold tinsel and handed it to Nan.

For a moment her heart almost stopped—an engagement ring! Of course not. The village store stocked practically everything, but not jewellery. Nan unwound the long strand of tinsel to reveal a pretty little enamelled pill case—the sort that a lot of their elderly women patients used to keep their tablets in. The local pharmacy sold them as a sideline.

'Oh, how pretty. It's a lovely present, Callum. I've got something for you, too, but you must wait to have it in the morning.'

She was almost tempted to fetch the little glass dragon, which she had wrapped earlier with such care, from her bedroom but decided against it. No—later today. That would be soon enough. She wanted to savour the moment when he opened it, and she didn't want to spoil Callum's obvious pleasure in his present to her.

'I dare say I'll survive,' Callum said wryly. He nodded at the pill case. 'Aren't you going to open it?'

What could be tiny enough to fit into a pill case? She clicked it open and revealed a circle of surgical gauze sprinkled with glitter. Carefully she lifted up one corner and there, lying on a bed of cotton wool, was a silver ring with a brilliant oval green stone winking in the lamplight.

'It's only cheap metal and glass,' murmured Callum, lifting it out, 'but I thought it might do temporarily till we can get the real thing—rather like a locum really, a stopgap till you can get the real thing.' He held the ring in the palm of his hand. 'Will you wear it for me Nan, please?'

Nan was speechless. Through a glaze of tears she stared at the shimmering glass gem and held out her left hand. Callum slipped it on her ring finger and kissed it.

He gave her one of his beautiful smiles and said in his throaty Sean Connery brogue, 'Not a bad little gift to come out of a cracker, is it? I did a swap with Peter. He didn't much care for it, thought it was uncool. He much preferred the racing car I had in my cracker.'

Nan laughed till the tears ran down her face and had to be kissed away.

'Stopgap or not, I shall never, ever swap this,' she whispered. 'Not for the finest engagement ring in the world. This will bind me to you as firmly as the most expensive ring money can buy.'

Callum kissed her again. 'What more could a canny Scotsman want?' he said. 'I have the perfect fiancée, happy with a Christmas cracker bauble wrapped in tinsel. I'm going to love and cherish you, Nan, for ever and ever, and that's a promise, dear heart.'

MILLS & BOON®

Makes any time special™

Mills & Boon publish 29 new titles every month. Select from…

Modern Romance™   Tender Romance™

Sensual Romance™

Medical Romance™   Historical Romance™

MAT2

MILLS & BOON

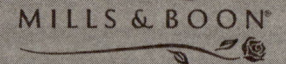

Medical Romance™

THREE LITTLE WORDS by *Josie Metcalfe*

Book Three in Trilogy

Dr Kirstin Whittaker had thought that her work with special babies was enough to satisfy her maternal instincts. Then one day she realised that she wanted her own—was Dr Sam Dysart the man to help her?

JUST GOOD FRIENDS by *Maggie Kingsley*

Despite their professional differences, Bethany Seton and Dr Michael Marcus couldn't deny their growing feelings. But with one failed marriage behind her, Bethany had no intention of risking her heart again…

THE PATIENT LOVER by *Sheila Danton*

Although new locum doctor, Liam Taylor, was the first man in a long time to stir Bea's heart, she was determined not to give in to her feelings. However, her daughter felt it was time that she did!

On sale 5 January 2001

Available at most branches of WH Smith, Tesco, Martins, Borders, Easons, Volume One/James Thin and most good paperback bookshops

MILLS & BOON®

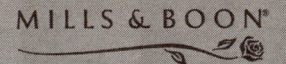

Medical Romance™

THE LOVING FACTOR by Leah Martyn

Dr Cate Clifford's new locum partner, Andrew Whittaker, was just the type of man she could fall in love with. Yet as their friendship deepened, she realised Andrew was not all that he seemed...

A LEAP IN THE DARK by Jean Evans

Life on the Island of Hellensey was just the way Dr Kate Dawson wanted until the arrival of Dr Sam Slater. Her divorce two years previously had shattered her trust in men but was Sam about to change that?

WORTH THE RISK by Sarah Morgan

New Author

Dr Ally McGuire and Dr Sean Nicholson were a formidable professional team. Neither was about to jeopardise their working relationship until, after one unexpected night of passion, Ally became pregnant...

On sale 5 January 2001

Available at most branches of WH Smith, Tesco, Martins, Borders, Easons, Volume One/James Thin and most good paperback bookshops

FREE

4 BOOKS
AND A SURPRISE GIFT!

We would like to take this opportunity to thank you for reading this Mills & Boon® book by offering you the chance to take FOUR more specially selected titles from the Medical Romance™ series absolutely FREE! We're also making this offer to introduce you to the benefits of the Reader Service™ —

- ★ FREE home delivery
- ★ FREE gifts and competitions
- ★ FREE monthly Newsletter
- ★ Exclusive Reader Service discounts
- ★ Books available before they're in the shops

Accepting these FREE books and gift places you under no obligation to buy; you may cancel at any time, even after receiving your free shipment. Simply complete your details below and return the entire page to the address below. **You don't even need a stamp!**

YES! Please send me 4 free Medical Romance books and a surprise gift. I understand that unless you hear from me, I will receive 6 superb new titles every month for just £2.40 each, postage and packing free. I am under no obligation to purchase any books and may cancel my subscription at any time. The free books and gift will be mine to keep in any case.

M0ZEC

Ms/Mrs/Miss/Mr .... Initials ....

BLOCK CAPITALS PLEASE

Surname ....

Address ....

....

.... Postcode ....

Send this whole page to:
UK: FREEPOST CN81, Croydon, CR9 3WZ
EIRE: PO Box 4546, Kilcock, County Kildare (stamp required)

Offer valid in UK and Eire only and not available to current Reader Service subscribers to this series. We reserve the right to refuse an application and applicants must be aged 18 years or over. Only one application per household. Terms and prices subject to change without notice. Offer expires 30th June 2001. As a result of this application, you may receive further offers from Harlequin Mills & Boon Limited and other carefully selected companies. If you would prefer not to share in this opportunity please write to The Data Manager at the address above.

Mills & Boon® is a registered trademark owned by Harlequin Mills & Boon Limited.
Medical Romance™ is being used as a trademark.